MW00848985

# THE
# FACT CHECKER

# THE
# FACT CHECKER

A Novel

# AUSTIN KELLEY

Atlantic Monthly Press
*New York*

Copyright © 2025 by Austin Kelley

All rights reserved. No part of this book may be reproduced in any form or by any electronic or mechanical means, including information storage and retrieval systems, without permission in writing from the publisher, except by a reviewer, who may quote brief passages in a review. Scanning, uploading, and electronic distribution of this book or the facilitation of such without the permission of the publisher is prohibited. Please purchase only authorized electronic editions, and do not participate in or encourage electronic piracy of copyrighted materials. Your support of the author's rights is appreciated. Any member of educational institutions wishing to photocopy part or all of the work for classroom use, or anthology, should send inquiries to Grove Atlantic, 154 West 14th Street, New York, NY 10011 or permissions@groveatlantic.com.

Any use of this publication to train generative artificial intelligence ("AI") technologies is expressly prohibited. The author and publisher reserve all rights to license uses of this work for generative AI training and development of machine learning language models.

This book is a work of fiction. Names, characters, places, and incidents are products of the author's imagination. Any resemblance to actual events, locales, entities, or persons living or dead is entirely coincidental.

FIRST EDITION

*Printed in the United States of America*

First Grove Atlantic hardcover edition: April 2025

Library of Congress Cataloging-in-Publication data is available for this title.

ISBN 978-0-8021-6410-0
eISBN 978-0-8021-6411-7

Atlantic Monthly Press
an imprint of Grove Atlantic
154 West 14th Street
New York, NY 10011

Distributed by Publishers Group West

groveatlantic.com

25 26 27 28 29 30    10 9 8 7 6 5 4 3 2 1

For Emily

# PART ONE
# KNOWN UNKNOWNS

# Chapter 1

# KALASHNIKOVS

It may seem odd, if not idiotic, that the story that took up so much of my time and energy, the story that was ultimately the end for me, was about food, not terrorism. This was 2004. Back then, I spent a lot of time on the phone with policy wonks and security experts, chasing down the truth about Al Qaeda and Abu Ghraib. Even when I was fact-checking a theater review, say, or a celebrity profile, there was always an offhand reference to Dick Cheney in it. So I'd have to look up something about Dick Cheney. Or Rumsfeld. Or W. Or about all the people in Iraq, dead and dying, perhaps dying at that very moment. The final straw, though, wasn't a piece about the dead or the dying or about the politicians sending people off to die and acting clueless about it. It was a food piece. But that's how it goes. As a checker, you don't choose what you check. You check everything. That's the calling. You have to pick and poke at every little assertion from every angle. And you never know, when you are picking and poking, what will ooze and leave a stain.

I didn't expect "Mandeville/Green" to be an oozer, though, not when Charles, the research chief, first dropped the galleys on my desk. I remember that day well. I was busy checking some facts about calcium ammonium nitrate, a chemical often found in improvised explosive devices, while waiting for a call from the widow of a CIA agent whose husband may or may not have been killed by an IED. I was on edge. Everyone was. Not that you'd know it if you walked into Checking. It was not one of those loud, fast-talking newsrooms. We were quiet. We were careful.

"Here's that farmers market piece," Charles said, almost whispering.

I didn't look up.

"It should be pretty simple," he continued. "Mandeville has all the sources."

I took the galleys and threw them on the pile. The phone rang.

"It says here you live in Chevy Chase, Maryland," I remember saying to the CIA widow. "Is that correct?"

"In a split-level house? OK, great," I continued. "The writer mentions some of the furnishings in your house. Is there a big rug in the living room? Right, that's the one. What color is it? So you'd say beige, not brown. It's a brownish beige? Uh-huh. So it's not wrong to call it brown? And do you know how big it is? Could you possibly measure it? You could? Yes, I'll hold on."

That's how I got the CIA widow, whose husband had likely been blown to pieces, to look through her closet for a tape measure. That's the kind of thing I do. I badger people about details, sometimes irrelevant details. True story: While fact-checking a piece about Shaquille O'Neal, I spent a lot of time on the phone with his girlfriend, asking questions about their life together: How many Superman motorcycles does he have? What's your typical Chinese take-out order? At one point, I asked her about the spelling of a tattoo on Shaq's stomach between his right nipple and his navel. "Hold on," she said, and she took off his shirt. "It's *LIL Warrior*," the girlfriend read to me. Shaq, shirtless, grumbled in the background while I made his girlfriend confirm the cases: "Capital *L*, capital *I*, capital *L*," she said. "Are you sure there's no apostrophe?" I asked. No, there was no apostrophe. I made the correction. Just as I made the correction on the CIA widow's rug. It wasn't a "fifteen-foot brown Afghan carpet." It measured nine by twelve feet. We changed it to "giant."

I might have let these little things slide—who cares about the size of the rug or the punctuation on Shaq's stomach?—but I knew from experience that some details, irrelevant in themselves, become more significant when they pile up. Think of it this way: Say your girlfriend doesn't like your beige rug. Maybe she doesn't even say that explicitly. Maybe she just calls it the brown rug when you've always thought it was beige. Maybe what she really means, you later realize, is that she doesn't respect you anymore. Of course, the "brown rug" comment in itself doesn't matter. We don't, like Sherlock Holmes, look at the carpet and uncover the philanderer. One "telling detail" doesn't tell us much, but a succession of dozens of details working in concert creates an impression, and impressions are sometimes as powerful as declarations of fact. She lost the earrings you gave her. She lied about her doctor's appointment. She called your medium-size beige rug a "little brown carpet" or a "shitty little carpet." Is it a surprise, then, that she's sleeping with her dissertation advisor? Maybe I'm getting a bit too personal here, but what I'm trying to say is this: When I had the CIA widow measure her rug, I really did want to know if it was a "fifteen-foot brown Afghan carpet with images of Russian tanks and Kalashnikovs," but I was also putting together a bigger picture so that I could make sure the impressions of the article pointed us in the direction of "reality" or "truth" or whatever you want to call it. Some sort of fairness at least. That's what a checker does.

And yet, I was also stringing the CIA widow along. I was specifically not asking her about her husband's mistress. Not yet anyway. "Did you grow up in North Carolina?" I asked the widow next. This was a fake question. The article did not mention her upbringing, and I was pretty sure she did not grow up in the South. She had a Baltimore accent, I guessed. It was an odd accent. But I made up this question because I wanted to make her a bit more comfortable. I wanted to get her talking freely before I moved on to her husband's extramarital affair. According to our article, the agent had a four-year relationship with another woman in California, a relationship the widow discovered only at her husband's funeral. In the article, the affair suggested his unreliability. "He kept secrets to the very end," the article said, "even from those closest to him." The CIA agent was a maverick. Some thought he was brilliant; others thought he was delusional. The writer didn't entirely pick sides. I was right, it turned out. The widow did grow up in Baltimore. She still had family there. She was a big Orioles fan. She loved Cal Ripken Jr. She was talking now. She was less guarded.

"Did your husband have a favorite T-shirt?" I asked the widow.

"Yes," she said, "the Dartmouth one. Mark went to Dartmouth."

"That's it," I said. "The writer says he often wore it under his collared shirts. Is that true?"

"Yes, he always wore that as an undershirt. He actually had a bunch of them. They were like lucky charms," she said. "That's the way he is," she said, "or was," she corrected herself, "superstitious."

"Do you know if they all had the Dartmouth motto, *vox clamantis in deserto*?"

"Yes," she said, "I think that's right. It means a voice crying in the desert. Mark used to say that a lot. It was like his mantra, and—"

The widow paused. "Now it really gets me," she began again. Her voice, which had been calm, cracked. "It really gets me," she said, "the whole time in Afghanistan." Her voice grew calm, distant. "Never mind," she said. "He's gone now."

"I'm sorry to put you through this," I said after a long silence. I could hear myself breathing. "I hope it helps that we are trying to tell Mark's story." I tried to sound soothing, calm. I still wasn't quite sure how I was going to ask about the marital infidelity. The writer had assured me that the widow had been open about it. She had told him everything. Some checkers might have just trusted his notes and not put her through the difficult recitation of her husband's secret life. It must have been horrible to find that not only had you lost your loved one, but he'd been lying to you, he hadn't been what you thought. Just when you want to hold on to his memory, that memory betrays you. Perhaps it could be comforting, though, in some way. It might help her move on, to say, "To hell with you, I'm done with you." Who knows how the CIA widow felt? In any case, I wasn't going to just trust the notes. That's not how we do things at the magazine. If we can, we go directly to the source, not only to check up on the writer, but also to gauge the source's reaction before publication. Sometimes I feel like Mercury delivering messages from Olympus. Charles calls these messages "controlled explosions." It's better to set them off before the piece goes to press, he says, to break news before it's in the news, especially bad news.

"So it says here," I said to the widow of the maverick counterterrorism expert, the one who had died in a real explosion, "that your husband had an affair."

"Yes," she said, "he did. Is that in the article?"

"It is mentioned," I said.

"I'd rather you didn't mention it," she said calmly.

"I'll speak with the editor," I said, "but I can't promise anything."

Silence.

"It says that the affair lasted several years," I said, "and you only found out at the funeral."

I could hear her breathe.

"I'm sorry," I said.

"I knew."

"About the affair?"

"Yes," she said quietly. "I told everybody I didn't know. I told them I couldn't believe it when she showed up. I acted surprised. Who was this woman? But I knew. Of course, I knew all about it. He was my husband."


That's the conversation I had right before reading "Mandeville/ Green" for the first time. It unsettled me. Interviews like that always do. When they're over, I feel a great sense of relief, almost euphoria, and a great sense of dread. It is an odd combination. It's like coming out of a movie in the afternoon or waking up hungover. It's hard for me to switch gears, to reenter the atmosphere of life. I think immediately that I've done something wrong. I review the conversation in my head, or, really, it's not that I "review" it. I'm not entirely in control of my recollection. My interview replays in bits and pieces without my consent, just as facts are always replaying in my mind—endlessly pinballing. It's a curse, really. It says the affair lasted several years. Did she answer that? Was he a big Ricky Gervais fan? Did he always wear that T-shirt? Did I get everything I needed to get? Did I ask her about the dog?

That post-interview feeling, slightly paranoid about what I know or don't know, about what I said or should have said, is always bubbling under the surface for a fact-checker. I'm always drowning in a storm of information and doubt. But this feeling was especially strong that day when I first read "Mandeville/Green," and I think it was still with me, a few weeks later, when Sylvia disappeared. Maybe that's why I suspected something terrible had happened to her. Maybe that's what drove me to try to find her.

I walked over to Elizabeth's cubicle to talk through the CIA widow's responses. She was actually the lead checker on "White/CIA." I had to report my findings to her. It would help to get out of my seat, to break the spell of being on the phone with a stranger and asking personal questions. It would help to talk to someone, especially Elizabeth.

I was enthralled by Elizabeth when I first came to the magazine. She was the most trusted checker on the staff and had worked with just about everybody on just about everything. I had fled from my life as a history graduate student, and I was looking for something. I wasn't sure what. I was thrown directly into a big, complicated piece about a family of gangsters who owned an art gallery. It required many late nights in the office poring through court records and transcripts, working with Elizabeth. She and I interviewed criminals and artists and collectors. I even arranged for an inmate at Sing Sing to call me, collect, so I could interview him about an alleged fraud involving the painter Philip Guston. It was difficult, as you might imagine, to arrange an interview with someone in prison. We put it in a request and waited for the inmate to call. It was his choice. For days, while I sorted through hundreds of pages of notes and clippings, I never strayed far from my phone, hoping it would ring and at the same time fearing that it would ring. How would I even begin to talk to a gangster in Sing Sing about an abstract painter? We were under serious time pressure. We were working twelve-hour days. Everyone was always rushing at a weekly magazine, but Elizabeth never seemed harried. She never rushed. Rushing, she knew, caused mistakes. The prisoner did finally call and, despite my nervous stammering, I asked everything I needed to ask and got a lot of useful answers. I even managed to record his elaborate and detailed account of the Guston fraud, how he had cut and pasted from historical auction catalogs to fake provenance, and how he had held sham auctions in which he himself was the top bidder, only to later arrange a private sale to another bidder. He was happy to talk. He thanked me several times.

It was late on a Thursday night when we finally sent the piece to press, fairly certain of all the accusations and claims in it, some of which were quite damning to prestigious auction houses. Elizabeth surprised me by pulling a half-empty bottle of Wild Turkey from her bottom desk drawer and pouring us two large tumblers, neat. It seemed like we were playing out a scene from an old film noir, and for the first time in years I felt something like satisfaction. I was working on the side of truth. Not that my history dissertation hadn't been a pursuit of truth. It had. Occasionally, I even thought my research—about nineteenth-century utopianism—was important. But no one really wanted to read academic history. Even in academia, most people wanted sound bites and oversimplifications. As a fact-checker, though, my job was to prevent oversimplifications, to prevent distortions, to prevent lies.

But all this was long before "Mandeville/Green," in another millennium, actually. By the time I walked over to Elizabeth's cubicle with my notes on the CIA widow, the romance of those early days was gone. I still loved the nitty-gritty of checking, the careful weighing of facts, but checking came with its own compromises. Truth wasn't our only priority. Meanwhile, Elizabeth and I had settled into a friendly but distant relationship. Elizabeth seemed so impassive, so hyper-logical. Perhaps I did too. Magdalena, my ex, used to accuse me of that, anyway. I was too cerebral, she said, too much of a know-it-all, always complicating things and then lecturing about something random and arcane. Mr. Encyclopedia, she called me. I was always missing the point. Was that so bad? Thinking deeply? Putting things in context? Wasn't *that* the point? Maybe Magda was right. I certainly hadn't had any romantic relationships since she'd left me. I was stuck in my head. Now, looking back on everything that happened as I worked on "Mandeville/Green"—the mysterious pig roast, the killing of the sheep, the trip to New Egypt—I'm sure Magda would call me a fool. She'd think my obsession with finding the truth about Sylvia was just some misguided attempt at intimacy. But Magda was never very generous, and she was often wrong.

Elizabeth was on the phone, and I didn't want to bother her. So I returned to my desk, put on my headphones, and played some Willie Nelson. *Red Headed Stranger*. I'd just finished a profile of him, and I found his voice comforting. I read the galleys of "Mandeville/Green" for the first time. I didn't pick up my colored pencils or my Post-it notes. I just read. Nothing jumped out at me. Nothing told me that I'd end up passed out and bloody in the Pine Barrens. Nothing raised any red flags at all.

It's a food piece, I said to myself. It's not going to kill anyone.

# Chapter 2

# AN EDIBLE SAFARI

"Mandeville/Green." We referred to all not-yet-published stories at the magazine by the author's last name and a one-word description, or slug, as we called it. "Mandeville" was John Mandeville, a popular food critic. "Green" signified the article's subject, the Union Square Greenmarket in Manhattan. It wasn't exactly a puff piece, but it wasn't particularly controversial. It wasn't a political exposé. There were no secret sources. Instead, it was a mix of self-righteousness, cultural critique, and light comedy. The piece focused on a particular local farm, New Egypt, which sold trendy tomatoes, and was full of vignettes about farmers and shoppers, each with their big ideals and petty prejudices, at the Greenmarket. That's Greenmarket, one word, capitalized. It's a trade name used by the Council on the Environment of New York City, a nonprofit that founded the city's farmers markets in 1976. That's the kind of thing I check first.

I met with John Mandeville at the long table near the free-books bench. He was tall and thin with slicked-back hair. He wasn't extraordinarily handsome, but he had a quality, what show-business people might call a presence, or maybe it was just expensive skin-care products and spa treatments. His whole look—deep tan, coiffed hair, expensive-casual clothes—gave the impression of patrician ease. He reminded me of a young William Powell in a screwball comedy I'd seen in which Powell goes fishing with Myrna Loy and pretends to be a casual fisherman in order to spy on her, but of course he can't help being William Powell, a movie star. I don't remember anything else about the movie except for the title, *Libeled Lady*. That's the kind of thing a fact-checker remembers. Mandeville greeted me with an eager handshake. He seemed genuinely happy to see me. I was genuinely happy to see him too. I liked him.

I easily excused him, then, when he didn't have an annotated version of "Mandeville/Green." All writers are required by our department to annotate their stories, sentence by sentence, and to provide interview notes, tapes and transcripts, printouts of articles, books, page numbers, lists of phone numbers and addresses, even of secret or anonymous sources—every source for every fact. New writers are often intimidated by our department, which is understandable, since we, despite our sincere attempts to help, must be suspicious of them. It's not that journalists are liars (although some are), or that they are sloppy or careless or dumb (some are those things too). It's that everyone makes mistakes without realizing it. We all have inclinations that color our thinking. We all tend to believe certain people over others; we tend to read certain words and ignore others; we tend to confirm our ideas rather than to challenge them.

I had worked with Mandeville many times. He was not a liar, but he often left out large swaths of truth in order to give his story a more surreal and dramatic quality. The trick, in checking him, was to know enough of that hidden truth so that you could be sure that nothing and no one was grossly misrepresented. Mandeville himself was easy to work with, even if he was not that helpful or responsive. He would lose numbers and documents and promise to look for them but would never find them. As soon as he started fumbling through his notes, I knew I would have to track down the number or address or fact myself. Still, I wasn't concerned, at first, when Mandeville didn't have the last name or contact info for "Sylvia," the vendor who supposedly said there was "nefarious business" at the market. "People sell everything here," the vendor said. "It ain't all green."

"Sylvia something," Mandeville said when we reached my pink Post-it note on page three of the galleys. "I'm sorry, I should have gotten her last name. She works at New Egypt. I have their number here somewhere." He began leafing through his notebook. I wrote "Sylvia/New Egypt/Nefarious?" on the pink Post-it, knowing I'd have to find the number myself.

"Trust me," Mandeville said.

*Trust me.* This gave me pause. The quote wasn't in itself a big deal, even if it was an anonymous source making a damning accusation. It was vague. No one would sue. But I couldn't just trust him. There was something planted in the back of my mind, even then, about this innocuous fact. "Nefarious business"? It was one of the only dark moments in the whole piece. Mostly the farmers market was portrayed as an ideal and an idyll. What purpose, then, did this anonymous quote serve? Did it excuse the reader from too much utopianism? We urbanites could say, "of course the market isn't perfect. You and I know how things really work, Mandeville. It's the Wild West here in New York. Anything goes. We aren't like these hippie dreamers in the piece who are all a bit silly. They have unrealistic notions." The reader could be entertained and reassured. He could support the cute little farmers and still understand the wildness of city life, of capitalist life. Maybe that was all we could hope for, a little dollop of idealism on the shitty sandwich of life.

I might have pressed Mandeville about this, but I didn't. I was immediately distracted by what he did next. Mandeville moved his head closer to mine and looked around as if he were about to let me in on a secret.

"Sylvia," he said, "I think you'll find her—"

He paused and looked left and right. Then he looked directly at me.

"—interesting," he said finally.

It was an odd thing to say, or at least an odd way to say it, and it stopped me. It might have been a euphemism. Maybe he meant "she's a complete idiot" or "she's totally insane," or it might have been a sexual hint, "she's beautiful" or "sexy," or something more vulgar, "she has incredible tits" or "wait till you see the ass on her." I wouldn't have put this past Mandeville. He was a bit crude at times. And the way he looked left and right before saying "interesting" did seem like the actions of a man about to engage in "guy talk," to say something that he would not care to say in mixed company. I always resented such confidence even if I might also think the woman in question was attractive and might have considered her body parts. Still, this time Mandeville's words struck me as a thoughtful message, as if we were close friends and he knew my predilections—not just my "type," but something deeper. Mandeville and I, I thought unconsciously, understood each other.

It's odd that I'd react this way, since there were a number of things about Mandeville that made me distrust him. In addition to his aristocratic air, he had a careful, affected way of talking, like a poet or a seminarian. He seemed to be trying too hard to empathize, which was especially suspicious because Mandeville was known as a rake. He threw lavish parties in his SoHo loft where artists and models and disparate celebrities would eat sea urchin, or snake, or game Mandeville had hunted himself, and drink until dawn. Mandeville was reputed to be a heavy drinker, and in his first book, *An Edible Safari*, a mixture of anthropology, travelogue, cookbook, and hunting adventure, he drinks mind-boggling amounts, so much that if I had fact-checked the book, I would have questioned whether one could drink that much and survive. But I don't know who, if anyone, checked *An Edible Safari* (publishers very rarely fact-check books) so I cannot vouch for the accuracy of the alcohol consumption. Mandeville's reputation, in any case, put me on guard. One cannot be macho without being a bit monomaniacal and perhaps disingenuous.

Nonetheless, when Mandeville told me I'd find Sylvia "interesting," I was immediately intrigued. Perhaps I was just fooled by his charisma or by his spa treatments or by his slicked-back hair. I was surely making too much of his words, I thought. Then he repeated himself.

"You must talk with Sylvia," he said. "You'll find her very interesting. Go see her. You must."

# Chapter 3

# HUNTER-GATHERERS

That evening I stopped by the coffee shop Grounds Zero near my apartment and pulled out my "Mandeville/Green" galleys and documents. Mandeville had given me background materials, including a booklet by the founder of New Egypt Farms, Jack Jarvis, who was supposed to be a visionary, or a quack, or both. I didn't really need to be working on the story yet. I didn't need to be working at all. But I didn't feel like going to any of my usual bars like Sweetwater or the Ale House, and I didn't feel like being home, alone.

The coffee shop was filled with young, attractive people looking at one another drink coffee. Some chatted, but more often they read alone, or even more often they displayed themselves reading, perhaps, Jack Kerouac or Susan Sontag. Sometimes I'd get up on my high horse and complain about this performative reading. I didn't think books or ideas should be turned into fashionable accessories or badges of honor like tattoos. I didn't like tattoos—surfaces trying to appear deep. But who was I to complain? I was there too. I was often there, checking facts after hours and wondering about the other coffee drinkers, particularly if they were attractive women. In fact, I was distracted that evening by a woman sitting near the window, partly blocked from my vision by the service counter. I thought I knew her.

\*   \*   \*

I could see only the woman's hair and her shoulders, but she reminded me of Magdalena, my ex. I often would think, or not think exactly but sense, that I spotted Magdalena out of the corner of my eye. It wasn't conscious: My body would be pricked to attention. Some mixture of fear and excitement, a mixture Magdalena would have called a "fish," a fear and wish combined, would come over me. These phantom women were never Magdalena, of course. She was living in Palo Alto now and had a daughter and was doing well, or so I heard, even if she had married a charlatan. Not that it was my business anymore.

Jack Jarvis's booklet, meanwhile, was full of overblown messianic rhetoric that reminded me of the nineteenth-century utopians I'd studied in grad school. "Americans are alienated from the natural world," he wrote. "They go to the supermarket and walk through these corridors of doom. They don't know where they are. At our institute we want to restore the connection to the earth. We want to eliminate the deadening supermarket and regrow our roots. This is the only way to heal our broken society." This was followed by a lot of discussion of manure.

Was this the only way to heal our broken society? Could we heal it with manure?

I decided to get a better look at the Magda-like woman. I needed a coffee refill anyway. One of the nice things about the coffee shop was the free refill policy. But when I got up to the counter, I still couldn't really see the woman, so I inched over, and just as I did, she turned and looked at me. She did look a bit like Magda, but it wasn't her. It was the Fat Albert Girl.

I didn't know her real name. I had run into her once at Tops, the Polish grocery store on my block. Really, she had run into me. I was looking at the Asian pears, which were piled in a high pyramid, a structure so perfectly poised that I was almost afraid to touch it when someone bumped into me forcefully from behind and I fell into the pears. I tried to catch them, but I just flailed wildly. When I turned around, I saw this young woman, a woman who looked like Magda, smiling at me blankly. She was wearing an oversize blue sweatshirt with the words "Fat Albert" written in graffiti-like scrawl above car-toon images of Bill Cosby's Junkyard Gang (including the fellow with the hat covering his face, who is called "Dumb Donald"). I apologized profusely while she continued her otherworldly but vaguely friendly stare. Then we rebuilt the pile of Asian pears, silently. We just handed each other fruit. After that, I'd see her around, usually at Tops. We wouldn't speak to each other, but we made eye contact, friendly but distant contact, like neighbors in New England. I was intrigued by her. If I were Mandeville, I might have called her "interesting."

In the coffee shop she wasn't wearing any Fat Albert gear; she was wearing a long denim skirt and white shirt like a cowgirl—not an urban version of the cowgirl, but a dowdy cowgirl stuck doing chores. I thought about saying something, since I was now right next to her at the coffee shop. There is an unwritten rule, one of our magazine's critics had once told me, that you could never approach a stranger of the opposite sex whom you see all the time until you see that person in a different context. You might see a woman in the gym every day and say nothing to her, but if you see her in the grocery store, you can suddenly approach and say, "Don't I know you from the gym?" I was going to say something, but I lost my nerve (what would I say anyway?), so I sipped my coffee and looked out the window.

"Don't I know you from the Panic Room?" she asked me.

"No," I said. "Tops."

"Oh."

"Asian pears," I said, and immediately regretted it. I stuck out my hand to shake and immediately regretted that too. Shaking hands with an interesting woman rarely feels appropriate. It's almost like the very act of hand-shaking precludes the possibility of ever having a more intimate or meaningful connection. Your relationship is cemented into some formal transaction. Or maybe it's just me. I didn't like shaking hands with men either. She shook my hand vaguely and looked out the window. I wasn't sure how to keep up the conversation. It already seemed to have lost any natural momentum, and now I felt a twinge of guilt. My body conducted the same nervous energy that it does when I am interviewing someone. It doesn't matter whom: a Pakistani general, an innocent bystander, or a blind date.

"Do you live in the neighborhood?" I asked. It was a bland question, but I knew that most people, particularly New Yorkers, liked to discuss their living situations. It was better than asking, "What do you do?" or "Do you come here often?" and sometimes real estate could lead, through indirect means, into intimate terrain. Even bland questions, I knew, could be useful.

"Yes," she said. Then she paused. "Or no," she said. I looked out the window again and tried not to assign reasons to her ambiguity. It was gray out there. Bedford Avenue was ugly. "I'm about to move," she said, "maybe to Vermont."

"What's in Vermont?"

"That's where we—" she said. "David and I, well, he—" She took a sip of her beverage. I don't think it was coffee. Chai? I couldn't be sure. "Anything can happen," she said. She didn't look at me. I sipped my coffee and waited for something to happen.

"Like what?" I asked finally.

"What?" she said, confused.

"Like what can happen? You said anything can happen." I smiled, trying to cut the archness of my question.

"Well," she said, "what can happen?" She looked out the window and back toward me. "I'm hoping this dance performance happens in July, and, um . . ." She trailed off and looked out the window again like I wasn't there, and for some reason, instead of alienating me, this only made me more eager.

"Are you a dancer?" I asked. I liked dancers, or maybe I just liked the idea of dancers.

"No," she said, "not really."

"What do you do?" I asked. It was a lame question, but it came out.

She took another sip. I was pretty sure it was chai.

"Right now I'm working in vision therapy," she said.

"Vision therapy?" I tried to ask that in a way that sounded enlightened and interested, not confused and suspicious, but I may have overdone it, and it came out high and breathy and, I imagine, a little creepy.

"Yes," she said, "I work for a vision therapist. We work with kids," she said, "troubled kids, underprivileged kids. I love the kids." She smiled, but not at me. "We do exercises with them, on balance beams. We use eye patches and these different machines," she said. "We train them, one eye"—she put her hand in front of her eye, then wiped it away—"two eyes, then work with everything together, with coordination," she said, continuing a series of strange hand gestures. "I'm there three days a week. It's cool."

Underprivileged kids? I was fairly sure that was what I heard, but I couldn't quite understand what that had to do with vision problems. Was there some eye problem related to socioeconomics, or to diet? Did being poor in some way make you lose your balance? I was looking at her greasy hair and her faraway eyes and her weird cowgirl outfit. I wanted to ask her all these questions about the sociology of balance without sounding snide or incredulous, although in some sense I was both snide and incredulous. Eye exercises for underprivileged kids? Really? And if she was so attuned to vision, why hadn't she seen me right in front of her, shopping for Asian pears? Why had she been barreling through the grocery store?

"You're nearsighted?" she asked me.

I nodded.

"Take off your glasses," she instructed me. Before I responded, she reached over and took them off me with her rough hands. I was taken aback. It's rare that anyone, especially a stranger—especially a strange woman in a cowgirl outfit who looks like your ex-girlfriend—puts her hands to your face. "You work on a computer every day?" she asked. I nodded. "Do you ever get up and exercise your eyes? No? You should. Every fifteen minutes or so, you should stand up, walk around, and look as far into the distance as you can. Focus your eyes."

She was looking at me then.

"You see, thousands of years ago," the Fat Albert Girl said, "we evolved as hunter-gatherers. You know, everything was out there." She gestured out the window toward Bedford Avenue. "We needed to focus out there," she said. Then she put her hands right in front of her face. "Now we're reading or looking at computers," she said,

22

waving her hands right in front of her face. "Our focus is so short, but we weren't built for that.

"Stand up," she commanded. "Look outside. Look down Bedford."

I obeyed.

"Look as far as you can, at the very farthest thing, at the farthest traffic light, and try to really focus on it. If you do that every day, and you keep focusing, you'll see ten blocks, then fifteen, then twenty. Trust me, you'll get to see farther and farther." She smiled. I looked deep down the gray street. I tried to see as far as I could, but I couldn't see very far without my glasses, of course, and my line of sight was blocked by dark brick tenements. I stared at a traffic light. It turned yellow, then red. I tried to focus on it.

"You'll see," the Fat Albert Girl said. "Your vision will get better every day." She was up from her seat now. "And I think maybe it will help"

Help what?

"See you later," she said, heading for the door.

I put my glasses back on and watched the Fat Albert Girl walk down Bedford, turn left on North Fifth, and disappear.

I went back to Jack Jarvis and his revolutionary manure.

# Chapter 4

# EL GRECO'S

Early in the morning the Union Square farmers market looks dirty. The vendors are still unloading their trucks, and although the trucks are not idling and are not sending noxious black fumes into the humid air like so many other trucks across the city, they are still commercial trucks. They don't look clean, organic, or righteous. They look like your average small, semi-white trucks, invading one of the few vestiges of green in the city. At 7:00, most vegetables and fruits and homespun goods are not ready for the public. They are still being tossed and stacked in black, mud-encrusted crates, lined up by sweaty men and women like any other unnatural and possibly deleterious commodities. Or, at least, this was the perception I had of the market as I watched the vendors setting up on a grossly humid July morning. My perception may have been colored by my lack of sleep and my slight hangover. I had popped out of the subway on the south side of Fourteenth Street and immediately begun sweating. Then, as I walked north through the park in a mental fog, barely noticing the homeless or semi-homeless sleepers or the parade of strollers, I felt a great sense of relief. The path through the shade trees and shrubberies felt dramatically cooler. I sat down for a few minutes on an empty stretch of benches near an ugly blue hydrangea and breathed the air that seemed, at that moment, wildly less toxic than the air just thirty yards south. When I got up then and walked over to the concrete clearing of the market, the oppressive heat hit me again. I breathed the dirty air. As I watched those trucks spit out dirty crates of vegetables, I felt a little sick.

I had decided to stop at Union Square on a reconnaissance mission, which was perhaps ill-advised. I knew I'd have to go to the market sooner or later for "Mandeville/Green." Mandeville had told me that I might have better luck finding some sources in person at the stands than reaching them on the phone, and there were a lot of details in the piece, like the "hipster vibe" of the workforce at New Egypt Farms, or the "snarky comments" they often made about the tomatoes at Stokes Farms, the stall next to theirs, details that might be easier to witness in person. But that Wednesday morning was too soon. I had not yet prepared my full list of questions. I didn't know exactly what I needed to know. Plus, it was early, and I was sweating. I wasn't ready to get out my notebook and begin interrogating strangers no matter how "interesting" they were, especially if they were "interesting." I wasn't alert enough. But perhaps these were just excuses. I was always hesitant right before interrogations. Interviews were delicate affairs, especially in-person interviews. I had to be ready for all sorts of responses. I had to be ready for lies.

As I approached the New Egypt stand, I saw a young woman. I guessed right away that she was Sylvia. Did she seem "interesting"? I suppose she did. Among other things, she had a scar on her face. It looked vaguely like a harelip, although it was more to the side of her mouth. I considered the term *harelip*, and the image of a hare popped into my mind, a cartoonish image of a muscular rabbit, probably from the film version of *Watership Down*, which had terrified me as a kid. Was the hare a distinct species or was it some kind of rabbit? I'd have to look it up, I thought, when I got to work. And harelips too. Or cleft palates. Is that the appropriate term? I realized then that I was staring at Sylvia. I wasn't looking at the tomatoes or shopping or doing anything that might make me seem like a normal person. I felt like a creep, a sweaty, hungover creep. I had to do something, so I lurched at her abruptly, awkwardly, idiotically. I extended my sweaty hand and blurted out a greeting.

"Do you remember John Mandeville?" I said. "The reporter. I'm working with him. I'm the fact-checker."

Sylvia seemed unfazed by my staring or my sweating or my lurching.

"Of course," she said, "I know Mandy. Tall guy. Slick hair. Terrible cook." She laughed.

Mandy?

"Are you OK?" Sylvia asked.

I let go of the tomato I was holding, maybe squeezing. I checked my fly. Up.

"I'm fine," I said.

A jumble of questions popped into my mind: What did you mean by "nefarious business"? How did you get that scar? How do you know Mandeville is a terrible cook?

"Do you like it?" she asked me. "Fact-checking?"

I did like it, I told her. I got to become a mini-expert on something different every week. From Afghanistan to breakfast cereal.

"I even check poems," I told her. That usually gets people. "I know it sounds a little crazy," I said, "but I'm the poetry checker. And the cartoon checker." Sylvia raised her eyebrows.

"I ruined a poem recently," I told her.

26

"Ruined?" she asked. She was lining up tomatoes on the table in some very methodical way. Occasionally she'd swap one tomato out for another. There was something mesmerizing about this, but I don't know what. I didn't understand her method.

"How do you ruin a poem?" she said.

Practice, practice, practice, I almost said but I decided against it. Some pigeons fluttered behind me and then returned to their place. Nervous and persistent. Like little fact-checkers.

"The poem had a painting in it, an El Greco," I said. "That's the kind of thing I check in poems. If you describe a real painting or a real place or a real person, I check it. In this case, the painting didn't exist. Or, actually, the poet was conflating two different paintings. In one, Christ was being stripped and tortured. In the other he was ascending into heaven. They were very different paintings," I said. "The poet had gotten the colors and details all mixed up. He was surprised when I sent him some images. He told me he could really picture the painting he described, but he admitted that I was right. He was misremembering the whole thing."

"Did he have to change it?" Sylvia said. "Isn't that the definition of poetic license?"

"It was his decision," I said. "But he didn't want to publish the poem anymore. He said that he was very sorry but that it was 'ruined.' That was his word. I felt pretty terrible about it."

The pigeons pecked near my feet. They made that awful gurgling sound. My nausea rolled through for a moment and then passed. I breathed the humid air.

"I think it really freaked him out," I said. "It happens sometimes. People have some strong impression of something, sometimes something they really loved, and then I come along and poke holes in it."

"So you're like the arbiter of truth," she said. "Crushing the little lies we tell ourselves—"

"Not necessarily lies."

"Feelings, then," she said. She was inspecting two pinkish tomatoes. "Crushing our feelings."

"Yes," I said, "something like that."

She swapped out one of the small tomatoes for another, larger, darker one and then breathed a deep breath, finished.

"You don't look like a feeling crusher," she said.

What did I look like? I was dressed too formally, as usual, in a green collared shirt. I looked much older than my thirty years. Overly formal. Out of shape. Sweaty. Sylvia was cutting tomatoes. An ambulance screamed down Park Avenue. The pigeons kept pecking. The sun kept blaring.

"Whenever I see an El Greco painting," Sylvia said, "it reminds me of this diner in Boston called El Greco's. It was this cinder block hole-in-the-wall restaurant. I loved that place. I have no idea if El Greco's the diner had anything to do with El Greco the painter, but I like to think it was his diner. It was kind of a ghostly place, so it made sense.

Sylvia sliced a bright red tomato. She was bouncing on her feet.

"I can still taste the soup I used to get, avgolemono, lemon soup," she said, "but honestly now I'm rethinking it. I can't actually remember how it tasted. It's more a feeling I remember," she said, "the soup was like this comforting thing to me. Back then I was a total wreck. but who knows? I'm probably misremembering the whole thing like your poet was. It wasn't avgolemono, it was something totally different, and I was totally fine, not a fucking train wreck."

Sylvia offered me a tomato slice.

At the time I didn't care much for tomatoes. It was something about the texture. They could be watery or mealy or strangely, ineffably firm. So when Sylvia handed me that tomato, and I took it in my mouth, I can't help but remember it as a kind of revelation. It was sweet and strong and fleshy. It wasn't exactly a fruit or a vegetable. Wasn't it meat? I took another bite. It seemed the opposite of anything I'd ever called a tomato. It was so solid, and yet liquid at the same time. It tasted as if it had been distilled and reduced, as if some mad French scientist—I'm thinking of those perfumers they call "noses" who are experts in essences—had taken the essence of hundreds of tomatoes, boiled it down, and injected all of it into this little slice now in my mouth. It was very good.

I took another bite. Some of the juice squirted onto my green collared shirt. I looked at it, dumb. Sylvia took a brown napkin, walked around the table, and dabbed the stain on my chest. I felt like a child. Sylvia was tall and lanky and scarred. She hovered above me. She took away the napkin. Much of the juice was gone, but I could still see the ring of liquid. It looked like an old bloodstain.

"Was that a Ramapo?" I asked, still staring down at the stain.

Sylvia didn't answer. By the time I looked up, she had walked away. Maybe she'd gone to throw away the napkin, I thought, but she wasn't over by the nearest trash can. She must have gone to the truck. I couldn't be sure. My line of sight was blocked by the awning. It wasn't the last time she'd disappear.

# Chapter 5

# INDETERMINATE

I watched the truck for a few minutes, assuming Sylvia was inside it or behind it. Two other vendors were there, almost standing guard. They seemed to be watching me and whispering. One was an older man with a long, billy goat beard. The other was a young, handsome guy, probably Latino, in a purple T-shirt, purple bandana, and purple sneakers. There was something menacing about them. I tried to look past them, to look far into the distance as the Fat Albert Girl had instructed, to see how far I could see and then maybe to see farther. I knew it was silly, of course. I didn't believe the Fat Albert Girl and her "hunter-gatherer" theory of biology for one second. As soon as you mention hunter-gatherers, your credibility is basically shot, but I had quit smoking, and looking into the distance was something to do. I tried to focus. My headache came screaming back. I took out a notebook instead and started copying the names of varieties off the cardboard signs:

"Cherokee Purple," "Paul Robeson," "Brandywine."

Across from them a bigger box of tomatoes was marked, RAMAPO. REAL JERSEY TOMATOES! THE ORIGINAL! These were a central subject of Mandeville's piece, the newest trend in tomatoes. Everyone was buying them. It was a local tomato revolution. They did look somewhat like the one Sylvia had served me, but I wasn't sure. Everything about it, the taste, the shape, the flavor, like most memories, had lost its uniqueness. I struggled to bring it back. Was that one darker than these? I inspected them closely. While I was feeling the weight of one Ramapo, a nice, hefty one, Sylvia reappeared. She began unpacking tomatoes from a paper bag. They were unlike any of those on display. Some of them were small and almost black, more like radishes than tomatoes. She sliced a few and offered them to me, one at a time, pausing between each. I made sure to keep all the juice in my mouth. None of these tomatoes were sweet and overpowering like the red one. They were rich and minerally, like root vegetables. If the Ramapos had the crowd-pleasing sweetness of a Hollywood blockbuster, these seemed more like good foreign films. Slow, contemplative, weird. I wanted more. I wanted to eat them all day.

"I grew these," Sylvia said. "I've been testing a lot of different varieties, trying to find what's best for our soil and climate. These are just some early-season heirloom plums." She gave me another slice. I tried to eat it more casually. Sylvia told me about the growing seasons of different varieties, about the difference between determinate and indeterminate plants, about early blight and late blight. Some of this information was in the article, so I jotted notes. I asked a few other questions, mainly about Ramapos. Sylvia told me they were New Egypt's biggest sellers "by far." Check. She told me that a lot of people think they are the Jersey tomatoes of their youth. "But maybe they're misremembering," she said. "Like your poet." The Ramapo, she said, only goes back to the sixties, when biologists were developing a lot of new varieties at Rutgers. There were a bunch of new, big, sweet red tomatoes then, as they tried to maximize flavor, disease resistance, and consistency, but all these hybrids disappeared, Sylvia told me, when interstate shipping and longer shelf life became the big priorities. New, tasteless supermarket tomatoes took over.

"Over the past few years, Ramapos made a comeback," she said, "partly because of Jack."

"Jack Jarvis? The owner of New Egypt?" I asked, knowing the answer.

"Yeah, he is crazy about old varieties," Sylvia said. "He's nuts about it—I mean, really crazy." She turned her finger in a circle near her temple. I nodded. I'd have to check with Rutgers, and I'd have to talk with Jack Jarvis. But I already knew that.

"I think you told Mandeville," I said—I tried to slip it in casually—"that some of the business at the market may not be so"—I paused, unsure how to put it—"aboveboard," I said.

"Did he write that?"

"He quotes a vendor saying something about this, about how it's a tough business and not everyone is honest," I said. "He doesn't name the vendor."

"He told you it was me?" she asked.

I nodded.

Sylvia turned her head right and left as if afraid someone might be watching or listening. It reminded me of the conspiratorial way Mandeville had looked at me when he told me she was "interesting." I instinctively looked at the guy with the billy goat beard—he was walking toward us—then back at Sylvia. She met my eyes. I felt a nervous excitement.

"He didn't give any more details?" she asked. I was about to answer when Mr. Billy Goat interrupted.

"Sylvia," he said in a gravelly voice. "Can you help us with the zucchini?" He looked somber, like a nineteenth-century preacher. Were his eyes crossed?

Sylvia smiled. "Sure, Warren," she said. "Give me a second." He receded but not far, hovering like a drone.

"Listen," she said to me. "Can we talk another time? There's a lot to do at set-up."

"Of course," I said. "What's your number?"

"Sorry. I don't have a cell phone," she said. "I'm trying to maintain some freedom." I felt my phone in my pocket. Still there. She smiled and stepped closer to me. "Can you drop by on Friday at the close of the market?" she said quietly. "We can go somewhere else to talk."

"Friday, sure," I said, mimicking her whisper without meaning to. "What time?"

"Six thirty," she said. "And you can tell me what you think of these." She handed me a bag of tomatoes. It seemed intimate, almost flirtatious.

Or maybe I'm misremembering the whole thing.

# Chapter 6

# MEAT

That Friday Fatima and Niko, busy with a piece on Russian oligarchs, were late to our meeting. There weren't enough seats in the dim library for all twenty-two of us, so they hovered near the doorway. A few others had pulled in desk chairs or were standing by the stacks. I looked at Fatima's face. She had that zombie look. I had seen it many times at Friday meeting. She was near the end of something, and soon, she knew, she would have to begin something new. Fact-checking was an incessant cycle.

Charles was going through the schedule for the next four weeks, for the issues we called "new A" (going to press next week) through "new D" (going to press in four weeks). He rattled off slugs like an incantation: "Gross/Traffic," "Talbot/Divorce," "Anderson/Kurdistan." He came to "Mandeville/Green."

"It's coming along," I said, which was true enough. I'd gotten a lot of background checking done, but I still had to talk to Sylvia again and to her boss, Jack Jarvis, who was one of the main sources. I'd left him a few messages. No response yet.

"It's being held," Charles said. "It'll move to new B at earliest. But it might go at any time. It's one of those."

It's one of those. Meaning I should get it in the can as soon as possible because they'd want it ready, like a pinch hitter, if they needed to replace another story. But that also meant it would probably keep giving way to more urgent stories, which I'd also have to check. I'd need to cram "Mandeville/Green" in between things. In the next breath, Charles assigned me the A issue Prelude, a short opinion piece that would need to go to press by the end of the day and would take all precedence. Often it didn't arrive until midafternoon, and it kept you late. I thought about objecting. I already had a lot on my plate: the Tony Curtis piece, "Johnson/Memorials," the Murakami fiction, and a 6:30 date with a "Mandeville/Green" source who'd mentioned some "nefarious" activity at the Greenmarket. But those were not excuses. If I had to be late for Sylvia, I had to be late for Sylvia. Deadlines are deadlines.

Charles moved past D week and into the foggy future, where some stories were still little more than slugs—slugs that might never develop. "Maxwell/Fresh Kills," he said. "Parker/Swift Boat," he said. "Redonda/Meat," he said. "I'll take it!" Sam shouted. There was a chorus of laughs. "Redonda/Meat" had been on the schedule for more than a year, and no one had seen a word of it. Each week it would be pushed back, never cracking D week. We all liked hearing Charles call "Redonda/Meat." It released us momentarily from the incessant deadlines, from the feeling that we were all constantly chasing a mounting pile of facts, all potentially wrong, without time to breathe or think or make sense of any of it. I felt a little sad, though, for Redonda, whoever she or he was, whose story about some unknown property of meat was always on the horizon but never appeared.

When Charles finished with the schedule, Mr. Lancaster began to introduce new books for the checking library. Everyone tensed a bit. Mr. Lancaster was a frail old ghost of a man. He had been wearing the same threadbare blue blazer to the office for twenty-five-plus years. One of the few tasks he still performed was obsessively stocking our library with esoteric reference volumes, which he liked to introduce slowly, methodically, pointlessly. We all had more important things to do that Friday than to hear about useless books, but we remained silent and respectful. We treated Mr. Lancaster the way one might treat a venerated but senile old uncle.

"It's from the Vanguard series," Mr. Lancaster was saying in his slow, overly fastidious manner between deep, unhealthy smoker's breaths. "I think we have one or two of these books in the library already," he said, "so you may be familiar with how they are laid out. This one is called *American Civil War Artillery, 1861–65*. It's by Philip Katcher, with illustrations by Tony Bryan. There are two volumes. The first is *Field Artillery* and the second is *Heavy Artillery*. You can see here"—he demonstrated—"if you needed information on, say, the twenty-four-pounder siege gun and carriage, you would see that it was the heaviest maneuverable American gun and carriage, weighing ten thousand one hundred fifty-five pounds including limber and requiring ten horses to pull. It could penetrate eight feet, six inches of old earthworks at one hundred yards. Here is a picture of the cannon." He waved it around like a schoolteacher. "These books," he said, "will be in our military section at the back of the library." He pulled out another book and coughed.

A month or so earlier, Mr. Lancaster had checked a piece about the hip-hop artist 50 Cent. It was odd. Mr. Lancaster rarely checked stories anymore, and when he did, he usually worked only on classical music pieces. I suppose the department must have been stretched, and Charles must have called on Mr. Lancaster to extend himself. The story was written by one of Mr. Lancaster's favored journalists—he only worked with a few writers—so perhaps he had actually volunteered for it. Whatever the case, I didn't realize he was working on a hip-hop piece until I overheard him—we all did—on the telephone, asking someone in his slow, careful manner: "Is it 'motherfucker' with an 'e-r' at the end?" He spelled it out, m-o-t-h-e-r-space-f-u-c-k-e-r? His voice seemed to get even louder when he had to repeat the humiliating profanities. "F-u-c-k-a?" we heard him say. "Is that correct? Motherfucka?" He pronounced the end "aah" like a child is supposed to when the doctor is looking down his throat. I heard suppressed laughter break out in the farthest cubicle pod. Everyone else was absolutely silent, but Mr. Lancaster kept raising his voice as if he couldn't quite hear the person on the other line.

Now, as he was introducing another military history book, I couldn't help thinking of this moment and feeling terrible. Even though Mr. Lancaster was tedious and pedantic, I liked him. Maybe I liked him *because* he was tedious and pedantic. I liked our stiff and circumspect conversations about the Yankees or about nineteenth-century history. I even enjoyed his useless books. Sometimes, especially in the evening or early morning, I would page through books like *The Dictionary of Catch Phrases*. That's where I found the expression "He's gone for a Burton and gone for a shit with a rug around him," which means "He's missing. He may be dead." No one's quite sure, not even the writers of *The Dictionary of Catch Phrases*, what a Burton is or where this expression comes from. It's absolutely esoteric, but it kept coming back to me later when I was looking for Sylvia. It just kept popping into my mind: She's missing. She's gone for a Burton and gone for a shit with a rug around her. Then an image of the CIA widow's rug would follow. Nine by twelve feet.

Those are the kind of details that constantly flood my mind, esoteric catchphrases and rug measurements, and I imagined they flooded Mr. Lancaster's mind too. Like me, he had been a history graduate student, and like me, I sensed, he had been disappointed by the academic world. Now we were both here in this refuge of trivia, hiding away in the checking library reading *The Dictionary of Catch Phrases* that were no longer catchphrases, that were inscrutable and meaningless. Perhaps, like Mr. Lancaster, I was tedious and pedantic. When Magda used to call me Mr. Encyclopedia, she didn't mean it as a compliment. "I wish I were dating a person and not an encyclopedia," she would often say. Magda would always use the traditional subjective. "I wish I *were* dating a person," she would say, not "I wish I *was* dating a person." She was very proper that way. Some thought she was pretentious. But of course, by fixating on her grammar, I was missing the point. As usual. Perhaps I was too much like Mr. Lancaster. I was receding from the world. Had I gone for a Burton and gone for a shit with a rug around me? A giant, shitty brown rug?

When I began graduate school, I was so eager. Magda always liked to tell the story of the second time we met. I accosted her in front of the library and ranted about the millenarian writings of the Black Shaker visionary Rebecca Cox Jackson so intensely that Magda was a little frightened, like I was some crazy millenarian preacher. Within a few months, though, my enthusiasm was gone, even as I grew closer to Magda. My classes seemed stilted. No one wanted to go out after. I felt, when talking to my colleagues, as if they were looking at something right behind me, something just outside my field of vision, something terrible. Maybe I just had the wrong idea of things. But what were my ideas? I wasn't under the illusion that my obscure research on nineteenth-century American communes would change the world. Nor did I think teaching liberal arts to privileged students was all that radical, or even particularly important. I didn't really have a grand plan when I arrived. I was studying all these weird utopian groups that blossomed in the early nineteenth century—the Shakers, the Oneida, the New Harmonists—groups that were trying to fundamentally reinvent their social and economic reality, but why was I studying them? What the hell were they supposed to tell us? What was the point of learning everything about a bunch of dead idealists, only to pick apart their crazy ideas and trace their failures? I shouldn't have been surprised that my colleagues were not that interested in the connection between communes, feminism, and furniture design; they didn't want to go on road trips to search for millenarian bunkers or, as I was urging at one point, to dig for a lost shoe factory built by French communists in upstate New York in the 1850s. My colleagues weren't game for amateur archaeology; they only seemed to care about their position in the field. Or at least, they were always silently sizing up yours. Antebellum? New Social History? Professional threat? By the time Magda left me for the Fraud, my grad school experience was already soured. In the end, I couldn't really blame her for leaving. I had one foot out the door. I couldn't really blame her for choosing Frank either. He was very smart and very charming—charming enough to appear on political talk shows all the time, justifying American exceptionalism. He was a smart, vain neoliberal sophist, ready to defend the killing of thousands. And to sleep with his students. And to lie about it.

Mr. Lancaster was now introducing the *Encyclopedia of New Jersey*, which I was hoping was the last new book. "As all of you know,"

Mr. Lancaster said, "I do not approve of New Jersey as a worthwhile subject of inquiry, nor do I understand why anyone would choose to live in a place so close to, yet so far from, the pinnacle of civilization, New York City. Nevertheless, against my better judgment, I have added this book to our library so that you can now learn more about such important cultural advancements as"—he flipped through the book—"Monopoly"—Mr. Lancaster almost laughed—"the popular board game, which, it says here, was invented in 1904 by an actress named Elizabeth Magie Phillips in order to promote the ideas of the economist Henry George. This George fellow apparently felt that rent income was causing social inequity, and this board game was supposed to reveal the truth. Hence, Monopoly." Mr. Lancaster closed the book. "This will be placed in our extensive New Jersey section."

Fatima was halfway out the door. I felt her anxiousness. Sometimes checking the Prelude could drag late into Friday evening. It was best to get ahead of it if I had any chance of getting to the farmers market on time. I had a 6:30 date with Sylvia—or an appointment, I should say—and she didn't have a cell phone, on principle. I was starving too, I suddenly realized. I'd forgotten to eat. The meeting finally ended and I hurried down to the cafeteria for a sandwich, tuna salad. Or so-called tuna, plus whatever they caught in those nets, shipped halfway around the world, bathed in mayonnaise, and slathered on industrial bread.

# Chapter 7

# A DORSET MANOR

When I got back to my desk I found the photograph that was supposed to accompany "White/CIA" sitting on my chair. It showed the CIA agent in front of the Pyramids. The caption, which I had to fact-check, explained that the agent, pictured with his wife on vacation in Egypt, was a "family man with secrets." I looked at it carefully. I didn't think it was the CIA agent's wife in the picture. She was supposed to have sandy hair (although this detail was not in the piece; I'd read it elsewhere), and this picture showed someone with dark hair, and she didn't really seem like the woman I had talked to on the phone. I didn't want to have to call the CIA widow back again, though, to ask if this was a picture of her or another woman. How would I ask? I felt a little sick to my stomach. Maybe it was the tuna. I put the half-eaten sandwich down and took the photo over to Hannah, the art assistant who was working on the piece. I was hoping she had more information.

Hannah was pale and thin and pretty. But something about her made me uncomfortable. Her skin seemed almost translucent, like skim milk. And her long neck seemed too thin to hold up her head. She might just collapse at any time. Or so it seemed. Sometimes.

Hannah and I were friends of sorts, although our friendship had been made awkward by one evening some months earlier, when we went on a "date". I put the word *date* in quotations because it was another one of those meetings that wasn't technically a date. Since Magda and I broke up, I always seemed to be going on dates like this. I'd head out to meet a woman, presuming that she was romantically interested in me, to find that she was only interested in talking about her boyfriend or husband or someone on whom she had a crush, someone who was definitely not me. I would quickly deduce that my companion never considered our meeting for coffee or a drink as a romantic prelude, or that she had a very dysfunctional way of courting or flirting. Other times, I'd go to an event that was surely not a date, or so I thought—it was only a quick fact-checking meeting—and then it seemed like I was being interviewed. I always misread the signs. Or perhaps the signs weren't clear. Perhaps that was just the nature of being single in New York, at least among the educated, bookish types I knew. There were no signs. Everyone was tentative and ambiguous, like Magda had been, in her way.

As for Hannah, the art assistant, our ambiguous evening had begun on one of my "rounds." I had the tendency to pace around the office when I was thinking something through or needed an escape from my cubicle. I'd go on little errands to the editors' offices or the art department or, most often, to the magazine library. (We had our own fact-checking library, but the magazine archive was on the opposite side of the floor.) Hannah, who was the newest occupant of the art assistant desk (her position didn't even merit a cubicle), always liked to chat if I passed by. I wasn't sure if she was flirting or just friendly or bored. During one of my rounds, we discussed Billy Bragg, the English folk singer, and she invited me to his show. Someone had just canceled on her. She had an extra ticket, and none of her friends could go. In truth, I liked the idea of Billy Bragg more than I actually liked the experience of listening to Billy Bragg. As a graduate student, I was allied with Marxists, and Billy Bragg was part of my team. But even back then, I must admit, I could never fully subscribe to a comprehensive belief system. I always had doubts, and I found Billy Bragg occasionally too strident and self-satisfied, and his voice would begin to grate. I was also aware that he lived in a multimillion-dollar house in a conservative hamlet in Dorset, which made me distrust him. This was a problem I had. Maybe it was my central problem, an inability to commit, totally and fully, to anything without picking it apart, without doubting it. I had spent a lot of time in grad school picking apart utopian idealists and their failed experiments in living, and even though I admired something about them, I knew I would never have joined them. I couldn't really imagine joining up with anyone on any grand and unifying venture. When I listened to Billy Bragg, in any case, I did so skeptically while mulling over his flaws and inconsistencies, rather than simply enjoying his music or ignoring him outright. But I didn't feel like explaining my mixed feelings to Hannah, who was a fan. I said sure, I'd buy the ticket from her. We'd meet at the show.

Billy Bragg was quite loud, I remember, especially for a so-called folk musician, and so, although I was standing right next to Hannah and occasionally we looked each other in the eye, and sometimes we shouted to each other, we might as well have been in different time zones. Or, that's not exactly true. There is always an awkwardness on dates, and maybe this is heightened at concerts or movies or other places where talking is limited, so one only has one's interior monologue with which to navigate, and maybe it's heightened even more on "dates" that might not be "dates" or when you're not sure whether you want them to be "dates." There is an awkwardness of indeterminacy. The date may progress; it may change course. Feelings may ebb and flow. But you can't be sure, and you can't do much about it. You can only watch and listen. I watched and listened and smiled at Hannah, a smile that, I think, was friendly and noncommittal. She smiled at me in a similar way. I drank, and she drank. We drank a lot.

After the concert, we went to a bar with a jukebox filled with classic 45s from the 1950s and '60s, some of which I'd never heard. I found Willie Nelson's "Crazy" and "Hello Walls" and played them. I bought Hannah another drink. I don't remember much of what happened after that. I'd spent so much time during the concert silently thinking, wondering exactly where I stood and where I wanted to stand with Hannah, whether she might find me "interesting" (and, to a lesser extent, whether I might find her "interesting") and getting progressively deafer from the loud folk music that, by the time we actually did talk, we were both in a strange drunk dream state. At some point, Hannah began crying. She was worried about her brother, I recall. Drugs. "Your story really helped me," she said. "Thank you." She hugged me. I wasn't sure what story I'd told. I touched her shoulder, awkwardly. She was sweating and crying. Her brother had left rehab, but now he was probably back on heroin. He wasn't answering his phone. I patted her shoulder. She cried. "Worry," sang Willie Nelson, "why do I let myself worry?"

The next thing I knew she was flipping me the bird. We'd stumbled over toward her apartment building. We were about to kiss, I was sure, under the strangely yellow streetlight. I was wrong. Instead, Hannah pulled away from me, reached her door, turned, and gave me the finger. I remember this image: her wet face in the yellow

44

light suddenly flush with anger. I must have said something or done something that bothered her. Or maybe she was just out of her mind. She didn't say anything. She just stuck up her middle finger, turned, and went inside.

We never talked about our night together again. It just sat there in the background at the office, unspoken. I thought about that as I stood there with the image of the CIA agent with his wife or his mistress, hoping that Hannah could solve my dilemma quickly so that I could make it on time to the farmers market to meet Sylvia. I couldn't ask Hannah what the hell she meant when she flipped me the bird. Maybe she sensed that I was hesitant, that I was doubtful, even as she was opening up to me, baring her soul. I was removed. And this was a breach of trust, I thought, although I was probably wrong. I was being ridiculous. What trust?

"This is his wife, not the mistress," Hannah said. "His wife had different hair then. I'm sure of it. I'll show you some other photos."

# Chapter 8

# MARQUIS GRISSOM

The sky over Union Square was a strange color, as if a bright purple light was shining through a gray scrim. Painted on the scrim were jagged clouds, darker gray but also illuminated and shaped vaguely like states (Virginia? Tennessee?). Looking up, I was suddenly struck with an overwhelming sense memory. I must have been about five years old, walking under the same sort of clouds and same sort of purple sky through a field of tall wet grasses and enormous mushrooms. I was coming home from a playground or baseball diamond, I think. The mushrooms were everywhere, glistening, wet, and moldy. Someone was picking them, the adult with me. It wasn't my mother or father, so it must have been my aunt Leah. I'm not sure. What I remember is feeling that I was in a strange place, somewhere near my home, yet utterly alien. It gave me a sense of freedom and of fear, the mixture of which was exhilarating. As I stood there in Union Square, those feelings came back again so powerfully that I suspected it wasn't a memory at all, or not a precise recollection, anyway. I didn't have many clear memories of my early childhood. I can't actually picture myself in the house where I lived until I was seven years old. I only remember my later life in the suburbs. I presumed, then, that this strong image—the dramatic sky, the overgrown mushrooms—might have been cobbled from dreams or stories or many sources and unconsciously reconfigured as a memory. The sky in this pseudo-memory, I realized, looked exactly like those El Greco paintings, the ones in the ruined poem. But then again so did the real sky above me.

I didn't see any children playing in Union Square, nor any mushrooms. Those for sale had all been packed up and stuffed back into the semi-white trucks. Many of the food vendors had disassembled their stands, leaving big gaps in the market, a minor archipelago in a concrete sea. There was something sad about it, the dissipation of the market energy, the reconfiguration of the space, its emptiness. Or maybe the purple sky and my recollections were just casting a charged mood over the whole scene.

At the New Egypt stand I saw the guy with the purple bandana again and a gray-haired woman. There was also a man about my age or a few years younger. His bushy red hair curled around the sides of an old, stained Montreal Expos hat. I loitered at the stand for a minute or two, hoping Sylvia might appear. I wondered if she had forgotten our appointment, or if she had already left. But I was only twelve minutes late. Sylvia couldn't have left yet. I wandered around toward the back of the truck and back to the tables. No sign of her. Purple Bandana was watching me; so was Expos Hat. He was packing boxes behind the central table. I considered walking away.

"Is Sylvia around?" I asked.

Expos hat shook his head. "Are you a friend of hers?"

I paused for a moment. "Sort of," I said.

He didn't add any more info. He just kept packing up.

"Are you an Expos fan?" I asked.

Expos Hat didn't say anything. Maybe he didn't hear me, but the look he gave me wasn't friendly. It's closing time, I thought. I'm sure he's tired of dealing with customers all day, asking stupid questions. Mandeville had described a lot of silly, demanding customers at the market. But something made me feel like he was being more territorial, like he was guarding Sylvia.

"It's a strange hat," I said. "The Expos hat. I've always wondered about the symbol on it." The Expos hat had indecipherable cursive letters in different colors. "Do you know what that 'e-l-b' is?" I asked. "Is it French?"

"'E-l-b'?" he said. He took off his hat and turned it around. "The whole thing is supposed to be an *M*, for *Montreal*," he said, tracing it with his fingers. "It's a weird capital *M*, you see, with the lowercase *e* and *b* embedded in it for *Expos baseball*. It sort of looks like it's written in toothpaste."

"Like that toothpaste with the separated colors," I said. "Aquafresh."

"Yeah. It's totally Aquafresh," he said. "The colors are from the French flag: red, white, and blue."

"Les Expos," I said in a poor imitation of French.

"Oui," he said. He pronounced it in the droll way I recognized from French New Wave movies. He picked up a box of onions. "Sylvia should be back soon," he said, and began loading the truck. I looked up at the purple sky. Purple Bandana looked at me. A man pushing a high-design stroller, the kind that seemed like it might turn into something else, walked by. I heard the girl in the stroller say, "But wasn't it summer before, Dad, when Mekky came?" She couldn't pronounce her *r*'s and said *summuwl* and *befuwl*. I wasn't sure who or what Mekky was.

"Yes, Bella, that was last summer. There's a summer every year," the dad replied. I caught a glimpse of the child, sallow and stringy-haired. I could see her thinking over this new idea, summuwl every year.

"I loved the '94 team," The voice startled me. I hadn't seen the vendor return. "That's when I got into the Expos," he said.

"With Moisés Alou?" I asked.

"Yeah, Alou, Pedro, Marquis Grissom," he said. I considered for a moment that wonderful baseball player's name: "Marquis Grissom." Was that his real name? (I checked it later: Yes. He was the fourteenth child in the Grissom family.)

"I was in high school," the Expos fan continued as he packed more onions. "They had, like, the lowest payroll in the league, but the best record. Then, of course, there was the fucking strike, and they just canceled the season," he said. He packed onions.

"Are you a baseball fan?" he asked.

I nodded.

"Baseball fucking sucks," he said, suddenly angry. He stopped what he was doing. "I mean, not the sport. I mean, the sport is fucking awesome. The league, man, you know? Look at how they fucked the Expos, man."

I laughed. The Expos guy looked around. No shoppers. He moved closer to me, excited.

"They got screwed," he said. "They got the old screwdriver right up the ass," he said, imitating a screwdriver with his hands in a way that was unmistakably vulgar. "The league bought the fucking team, you know, just to fucking kill it. But it wouldn't goddamn die. They made a goddamn playoff run, the fucking Expos. It was like Jason or Freddy or some shit. They should make a horror movie out of it, *Night of the Living Goddamned Expos*. Then you know what the league did? The league cut their dicks off. They wouldn't let them bring up players from the minors. We won't goddamn let you fucking compete. That's what they were saying. We don't want you to have a fucking chance. You're dead." He now had two onions in his hands and was waving them up and down. He continued his rant about baseball, adding something that I couldn't quite follow about the Sherman Act and antitrust legislation. Centralized control, the Expos vendor was saying, was stifling freedom and competition. He was getting more excited as he lectured. He reminded me of guys I knew in college who loved to argue vehemently about states' rights or the Balkan wars or whatever they'd just read about. I never liked arguing. "And now," he said, "whenever one of the little teams innovates, and figures out some other way to win games without big money, the league just fucking steps on their dicks, you know." His profanity had gotten stronger and more creative as he continued. "Well, bull-motherfucking-shit-in-the-dick-hole," he shouted. "That's bullshit."

Out of the corner of my eye I spotted Sylvia sliding toward us in the purple-gray evening.

"I mean, is the government forcing all these people to come down here and eat locally grown onions, man?" the Expos fan was saying. He didn't see her behind him. "No. They've got their heads up their shitholes," he said. "But people are still coming here, dude."

He didn't notice Sylvia till she was right beside him. "Hey, Sylv," he said with a sheepish grin, as if caught stealing candy.

"Hey, Nick," she said. "Hey, fact-checker."

"You're a fact-checker, man?" Nick said. Then he added quietly, as if he were thinking deeply about a personal memory, "That's cool."

Nick turned to Sylvia, excited again. "Did you get the stuff?" She nodded and patted a small brown paper bag.

"Give me two minutes," Sylvia said to me, and they both disappeared into the back of the truck with the brown paper bag. I had no idea what "the stuff" could be.

I watched a pair of skateboarders trying to take back the concrete from the Greenmarket. One of them was wearing an acrylic skullcap despite the July heat. It must have been like a uniform. He kept trying to pop his board into the air, perform a kickflip, and then land on a parking barrier. I watched him fail. I watched him fail again. I watched him fail again. I wondered what sense of satisfaction he would get if he finally landed it. He'd probably try again, right after, and fail again.

# Chapter 9

# A DUTCH TRADING SHIP

"Ah, yes, it's open," Sylvia said, pushing a creaky Gothic gate just wide enough for us to slip through. We had emerged from the R train at Rector Street and were presented with a large stone wall, which I now realized was the back of the Trinity churchyard. We were at a much lower elevation than the front of the church, at Broadway and Wall Street, so that we seemed to be in a deep canyon that cut through Lower Manhattan. It wasn't a particularly nice canyon. It was ugly and deserted. Across the street a big boring building said in block letters, AMERICAN STOCK EXCHANGE. I wondered how many lesser stock exchanges there were, how many aspiring capitalists performing minor acts of exploitation.

"Come this way, fact-checker" Sylvia said. "I want to show you something." She kept calling me that. She said it with great emphasis, pronouncing every letter, FACKT-CHECKER. Her voice was mocking but playful, I thought. Or maybe I was misreading it. I followed her up the dank stairwell.

I had no idea where we were going. When I met Sylvia at the market, she had asked me if I was hungry. I had assumed we would just grab a coffee or something, maybe she would give me some more tomatoes, and then she would tell me the things she had been holding back. She would explain this so-called "nefarious business" at the farmers market. So when Sylvia headed for the R train, I was slightly confused. Why were we getting on the subway? She rolled her eyes and raised her dark eyebrows. "Trust me," she said. I didn't want to seem unspontaneous or uptight, and, truthfully, I was hoping we might have a longer conversation. I was "interested" in her. Plus, I must admit, there was also something about her manner. She was mysterious but authoritative. Committed. So I didn't ask again. I just followed. I'd get around to my questions eventually. I had them all prepared. There was no point in badgering her. I would just see where things went.

This is where things went: to a graveyard in the Financial District, a graveyard that, I was pretty sure, was supposed to be closed, under an uncanny, darkening sky. Not that I was superstitious. I had always liked old churches and had no particular hang-ups about graveyards. When I was a teenager, I had a goth phase. I wore a black trench coat and listened to Bauhaus and the Cure, and I'd often go to an old cemetery near my house, a leafy and unkempt little place that fronted a brand-new housing development. I liked the weird juxtaposition of the two things. But this was all a teenager's self-conscious pose. That night in Lower Manhattan, I wasn't a teenager anymore.

I examined the worn-down headstones. Some of them were quite old. Those were the ones that caught my attention. Obviously people have been dying for thousands of years, and in some sense old gravestones and old deaths should be no more interesting than new ones, just as deaths in our country should be no more worthy than those abroad. All those dying in Afghanistan and Iraq should be no less real than those who die in our city, but they are less real. The old graves impressed me more than newer ones: a unique life in this very place so long ago, marked by scratches on stone. I tried to read a particularly old stone. Its text had caught my eye. The engraver had had no regard for where the lines broke or for what we call in publishing "widows" or "orphans":

HERELIESTHEXOF
OFRICHARDCHVRCH
ERTHESONOFWILLIA
MCHURCHERWHO
DEIEDTHE
1681OFAGE5YEARS

There was one line below this, but it had mostly sunk into the earth. Trying to read these things, I felt not like one joined in the repeated human cycle of life and death, but like an alien unable to cross the gulf of history. It was similar to the feeling I get watching old comedians like Harpo Marx, violent and silly in ways that make no sense to me. It was strange to be alive.

Sylvia gestured toward a stone nearby. "Look," she said. It was an unassuming rectangular slab laid out on the ground, less than four feet long. It read, in letters that were not centered (were engravers so sloppy?), CHARLOTTE TEMPLE.

"Who's Charlotte Temple?" I asked.

"You don't know who Charlotte Temple is?" Sylvia said, exaggerating her disbelief. "This used to be a major tourist attraction. When I met a fact-checker who was scrutinizing all the public memorials in the city, I thought surely he'd know something about this."

Had I mentioned "Johnson/Memorials"? I didn't remember that.

"She was no one, actually. She didn't exist. She was a character in a popular novel, *Charlotte: A Tale of Truth*. Ironic title, right? Then someone dug this grave and put her name on there. Maybe someone is buried here. Maybe not. Nobody knows."

"When's it from? There are no markings."

"The book was late eighteenth century, but the grave is a total mystery. Trinity's records were destroyed in a fire. But supposedly by the mid-nineteenth century people were coming here in droves. They left locks of hair and cried for Charlotte. It was all the rage."

Sylvia was now standing above the gravestone, feet on either side, casting a long shadow across the boneyard.

"It's weird. I read the book, only because I used to come here, and a priest told me the story. It's a dismal book. Charlotte gets seduced and abandoned and dies. But people loved her. People love a helpless woman," Sylvia said, "especially if she's dead or, like, totally made up, you know. There is so much fake sentiment out there. It makes real sentiment seem so hollow.

"Sorry," she said. "You probably think I'm crazy."

"No I don't," I said. "Or not yet anyway."

I looked closer at the simple stone. The grass around it was shabby and untended.

"It's weird," I said, "what people will decide to care about."

"It *is* weird," she said. "Like Ground Zero."

I was thinking the same thing. It was just a few blocks away. People from all over the country cared about that in a way that I couldn't understand, even though I saw the buildings burn. I knew someone who'd died in them, though I knew him only vaguely, a friend's brother's best friend. Really, I didn't know him at all. Sometimes I thought I should care about it more.

"Do you know there is a sixteenth-century Dutch trading ship buried beneath Manhattan, right by Ground Zero?" I said. "They found it when they dug out the subway there, in 1916."

"It's still there?"

Some of it is, I told her. There are beams from the ship in storage at the Museum of the City of New York, but the rest of the ship is still part of the island.

"The ruins of capitalism," she said to no one in particular.

I looked at her face. The scar blended into the shadows. She seemed to be focused on something. Not me. Maybe she was working on her eyesight. She began walking away.

"When I was a kid," Sylvia said—I was trailing a step behind her; we were near the cemetery gates on the Broadway side at this point—"I was always the skeptic. I grew up in a kind of crazy house. My mom was"—Sylvia paused and turned to me; I looked up at the sky; I had been staring at her neck—"I guess you could say, she *is*, a dreamer. When I was young, she was always making stuff up, telling me lies about everything. I mean real lies—she's kind of a compulsive liar—but also fantasy stuff that you tell kids. She would say things like 'The horse told me this' or 'The sheep told me that.' 'The sheep told me that you should be nicer to your stepfather,' she'd say. From a really young age, I'd get annoyed with this. I'd just shake my head. I'd be, like, 'Ma' "—and here Sylvia imitated herself as a skeptical child—" 'animals don't talk.' I hated my mom for that kind of manipulative bullshit," she said.

"So you're a natural born fact-checker," I said.

"I guess I hate lies," she said, "especially manipulative lies that are supposed to make you feel OK about something when it's not OK."

She looked over her shoulder.

"Should we go back there and dig up Charlotte Temple," Sylvia said, "you and I? You know, get to the bottom of things?" She had a playful look in her eyes. She was teasing me like an old friend might. For a moment I felt that I knew her and that she knew me. And yet we didn't know each other. A buzzing, a speediness, hit me, like the first time I smoked a cigarette, exciting, slightly nauseating.

I patted my pockets up and down as if looking for cigarettes, but I hadn't smoked in sixteen months.

"I forgot my shovel," I said.

I looked through the iron fence at Broadway. It was quiet. The sky was darkening. I took off my glasses and tried to look as far as I could, like the Fat Albert Girl had instructed. An old man rolled a shopping cart full of cans slowly past. I turned back to Sylvia. I thought about asking her about the farmers market. Why had she avoided the subject? What "nefarious business" could possibly be going on there? Was Mandeville's story full of lies, manipulative lies to make us feel OK about something that isn't?

But for whatever reason, I didn't ask.

# Chapter 10
# CAT POWER

We looped down Pine Street and around a little street called Exchange Place, which struck me as a command. Exchange places? With whom and why? Night was falling. I tried to gauge which way the river was, but among the narrow roads, it seemed the river might be anywhere. I was always turned around in Lower Manhattan. I followed Sylvia onto the loading dock of an old, unremarkable gray office building. At the top of the ramp, she took out a set of keys and opened a big metal door. We entered a concrete staircase and climbed the stairs. I had by this time given up on the idea of a quick coffee and was just following, eager, confused. We climbed the concrete stairs. The summer heat was trapped in the stairwell like a caged beast. It held me down, sweating. Sylvia bounded ahead. I looked at her calves clenching as she leaped upward. Her large, thin feet were bound by leather straps, vaguely gladiator-like, and I felt a sudden sharpness, imagining them pulled tightly against her flesh, like she was being tortured, like Jesus being flogged and disrobed in the El Greco painting, the one in which he wears a bright red garment, which the poet had described inaccurately. Sylvia stopped at the seventh floor and entered the dim hallway. "We're here," she said, and we went through an open door into an unmarked office.

It wasn't an office. Not exactly. The lighting was dim inside too, and it took a few moments for my eyes and my mind to adjust. Everything seemed out of context. The first thing I saw was a lectern, right by the door, a big old oak lectern, the kind they might have at a rustic-styled restaurant. To my right there were maybe a dozen mismatched tables, lined in rows and set out with place settings. Behind them was a makeshift bar, made from plywood and sheet metal, where a bunch of people, shadows to me, were drinking and talking. There was music playing somewhere, some kind of indie rock. It seemed like a weird restaurant, but also like a loft apartment. There were couches and bookshelves and end tables, some old Oriental carpets, and a huge thing (a sculpture?) made of what looked like vacuum cleaner parts, car tires, and steel beams. Surrounding it all were the trappings of a prewar office: massive ducting, old broken fluorescents, asbestos-wrapped support beams.

The lectern was empty when we entered, but quickly a tall, beautiful red-haired woman rushed to us. "Sylv," she said in the manner of an old friend. "Your new victim?" Sylvia introduced Agnes, who looked me up and down theatrically. "Your humble hostess," she said with an elaborate bow. Agnes led us to the bar. I began to make out the faces of a dozen or two twentysomethings. Everyone had asymmetrical hair and deeply referential fashion. There were Jazz Age outfits and New Wave outfits, differentiated in part by the color of the suspenders. Agnes, with her high-waisted green pants and tight jersey, was rooted firmly in the twenties or thirties, a time when Agnes was a more popular name. I was given a lychee martini.

"Paul always makes a signature cocktail," Sylvia whispered, but she didn't tell me who Paul was or where we were or what *always* could mean in this context or what she meant when she had told

Mandeville that there was something nefarious going on in Union Square.

Paul had a sort of jug-band chic: He sported a waxed mustache and brown suspenders. The drink was unbearably sour. I looked around at some blank faces and realized that my arrival had interrupted the conversation. I was struck by a middle-school awkwardness. Finally an actor named Davis in a red Bikini Kill T-shirt returned to discussing a version of *The King and I* he was involved with. It included puppets and was peppered with clips from Fox News projected on a big flag.

"It's sort of a mash-up about torture," Davis said. "It's a sensory assault on the audience." Davis seemed very serious about it, but his hair was carefully arranged to look messy, and he spoke with the self-assurance and overstatement of the thoughtless so I immediately wanted to ask questions about the play, to interrogate, as a fact-checker does. I was doubtful about the political usefulness of "assaulting" an audience of alternative theatergoers, but then I was doubtful about the political usefulness of everything.

"That's interesting," I said instead. "How long is it running?"

Marcus, who had a blond curly faux-hawk that extended down his back, was passionate about fermentation. He fermented everything and claimed that fermentation was essential to a healthy body and what he called a "strong life force." Fermented foods helped with digestion and boosted our immune systems. "It's like bringing the outside, all that vibrating life of the earth, all that biodiversity, right inside you," he said. "It becomes part of you." I sipped my sour martini and wondered if the earth was vibrating inside me. I didn't want it to vibrate. I looked around for Sylvia. She'd wandered off again.

The room had quieted slightly, and I recognized the music was Cat Power, a band about whom I had done some research a few years earlier. Back then I worked at *Rolling Stone*. It was my first fact-checking job right after I'd left grad school and Magda had left me. I didn't really know how to check facts, not well. The story, I remembered, was full of potentially libelous statements about Cat Power, who was really a woman named Chan (pronounced "Shawn") Marshall. I had to confirm details about her wild, erratic, and drug-fueled life, things that hadn't been reported elsewhere, including the overdose and death of her Atlanta boyfriend. I didn't have any record of the boyfriend's death or even of his life, I didn't even know his name, and it seemed wrong to mention his overdose parenthetically and not to find out more. But at *Rolling Stone* we didn't usually find out more. We checked everything off of interview notes or other press reports, or we asked the publicists. I knew that publicists, particularly rock- and pop-music publicists, were not very interested in accuracy. They were, in some sense, the enemies of facts. If they could get something wrong, they would. And later if this wrongness came to their attention and caused any difficulty or negativity, if a client wasn't happy or wasn't properly celebrated, they would be the first to complain. When you asked them questions, they'd say, "Yes, that all sounds right," barely listening. "Sure." Not that I had anything against publicists. They had their own jobs, their own pressures, their own fears.

I surveyed the room, looking for Sylvia again. She was always darting away, it seemed. I focused on a woman in the corner with short hair and a tank top. She was talking to someone whom I couldn't see very well but who, in silhouette—tall, with a dark swoop of hair and a shoulder tattoo—looked like Sylvia. She turned my way. Not Sylvia.

Davis and the others were now complaining about some mutual friend. He had the tendency to sing. He was always fucking singing, and it was endearing in a way, but he couldn't sing, and why was he always singing The Band. "Up on Cripple Creek" or "The Night They Drove Old Dixie Down." They were imitating him, whoever he was, imitating the singer of the Band, maybe Rick Danko or Levon Helm. I had backed out of the circle and sat alone with my drink. Cat Power moaned on.

I remembered how determined I was, back at *Rolling Stone*, to discover more about Cat Power's alleged boyfriend. After a long search, I found Chan Marshall's number and called her. I left a message, but she never called me back. I didn't keep trying. In the end, I failed to verify the facts about the dead boyfriend, and years later I read an interview with her and realized we were probably wrong. He hadn't died of an overdose but suicide, and he wasn't her boyfriend, just a friend. Now nameless and misremembered. I felt terrible about it. I had failed him.

I looked around the loft again for Sylvia. I wondered if Sylvia was anything like Chan Marshall—she looked a little like her—and now I was failing in my duties again. I hadn't asked her the most important questions. I didn't want to regret later that I had missed something important about Sylvia and about the Greenmarket, like I had missed something about Cat Power and her dead "friend." Where was Sylvia? Why had she taken me to the graveyard and then here and then left me with these hipsters?

Then I saw her. She was helping Agnes wheel a table into the middle of the room. On it was a pig's head. It looked wet and oily, almost like melting wax, and it suddenly made me think of the book *Lord of the Flies*, although I wasn't sure if that was just because there is a character named Piggy or if there was some deeper relationship.

"This is Siddhartha," Agnes announced to everyone, "our late, beautiful pig that we are lucky enough to enjoy tonight. Let's all take a moment and give thanks to him." She bowed her head. Everyone went quiet.

Cat Power's voice filled the silent loft. It was a dark and lonely sound. I thought of a woman in a barren landscape, in Scotland, maybe, a woman seeing and fearing death. Perhaps I was just under the throes of my overly sour drink. Or maybe it was the shadow of the trip to the cemetery or the dead pig in the middle of the room.

Paul raised his glass. "Hear, hear," he shouted.

"To Siddhartha," someone said.

We all toasted the dead pig.

"Hear, hear."

"Salud."

Agnes wheeled the pig table away. "Gotta get Sid back on ice," she said. "A head is a terrible thing to waste." Her green pants swooshed across the office floor. The glistening pig almost seemed to smile.

# Chapter 11

# MY LAI MASSACRE

The Heads and Tails Supper Club had begun with three friends, Agnes, Tony, and Goran, who all lived in that office loft. They'd moved in not long after September 11. It wasn't a squat, exactly, but it wasn't zoned for residential or for restaurant use, and they didn't have a lease. The manager took a monthly fee. It was only a few hundred dollars, but the building had been half-vacant even before the attacks and was now practically empty, so he was happy for whatever he could get. He told them they weren't allowed to live there, but he looked the other way when the "kids" (as he called them) built a shower and expanded the kitchen. He even helped them with garbage removal and with wiring and plumbing issues. They converted some of the nicer offices into bedrooms and built a living room and a small stage. It was an older office, in bad shape. Everything was chipped and cracked.

The Club idea came later after they'd been living there almost a year. Tony was a chef, and a woman (I assumed otherwise, to my embarrassment, even though I knew as a fact-checker not to make that assumption). She had worked briefly at Chez Panisse. The other two had no formal training, but they were foodies and they liked artistic projects and went along with it when Tony wanted to learn to cook offal and to cure meats. They invited their friends over to have a feast. Soon they launched the social club dedicated to eating holistically, as they put it, cooking whole animals head to tail and local produce grown by farmer friends like Sylvia. I gathered that Agnes was the impetus behind the whole project. She was in charge of the social part of the social club. An aspiring actress, Agnes seemed ready to perform melodramatically at any moment and expected the same from her guests. I avoided her gaze.

The first course was served while we were still at the bar. Crostini slathered with oil and small slabs of some kind of soft pink meat were set on big plates. I took a small one, afraid to give offense by taking more than my share or by not eating at all. It was deliciously salty and sour with a hint of hot pepper and an odd texture.

"Oh, yeah," said Marcus as he took a bite. "I also helped with the pickled tongue."

Tongue.

I was chewing tongue for the first time. It was remarkably similar to biting one's own tongue, I thought.

Suddenly flooding my mind: all the tyrants who have torn out the tongues of those who spoke against them. Saddam Hussein supposedly did this, as did American soldiers in Vietnam. "I cut out their tongues," one soldier said after the My Lai massacre. "Everyone was doing it." This was an exact quote. I had checked it.

But pigs were not people. And their tongues were delicious. I gulped down my martini and read the handwritten menu:

# *Heads*
### *&*
# *Tails*
### *Supper Club*

Three Little Pigs, Dinner #2

*Mahala's Backyard Bakery Crostini*
*Marcus's Pickled Pig's Tongue*

*Sylvia's Medley of New Egypt Heirloom Tomatoes*
*Sean Burke's Smoked Atlantic Sea Salt*

*Louis XIV Antique Offal Pie with Black Meats,*
*Anchovy, and New Egypt Cabbage Crust*

*Roadside Pigweed Salad*
*Pig Cracklins*

*Pork Five Ways*
*Bavarian Sauerkraut, Assorted Spicy Pickles*

*Pig-Out Pie*
*Ice Cream*

# Chapter 12

# DIONYSUS

Sylvia and I were the only ones who ate at our own table, slightly separated from the two main communal tables. Agnes had put us there, giving Sylvia a look as she did so, but I couldn't read it. Perhaps she suspected that we needed privacy, or perhaps we were unwelcome party crashers. Or *I* was. It didn't bother me. I was happy to have Sylvia to myself again, even if her presence was generally unsettling. She had changed her clothes at some point—when? While she was retrieving the pig's head?—and was now wearing a kerchief around her neck and this silky gray shirt with puffy sleeves. She was eating tomatoes voraciously, piling them up into large bites, and in that outfit, with her scar flashing and disappearing in the candlelight, she looked like some kind of ravenous pirate, not a real pirate in Indonesia or Somalia, more like *The Pirates of Penzance*. I didn't say anything for a while. I realized I was mimicking her—I was suddenly ravenous too—I had lined up green Striped Germans and red Brandywines and black cherries along the tines of my fork and stuffed them into my mouth. I washed it all down with a glug of red wine. Everything blurred together.

The music had changed. It was no longer Cat Power, but it was still something somber and folky. I tried to identify it. It was hard to hear over the scraping forks and knives and the party chatter. Maybe the band Smog. I looked down at the big helping of "offal pie" on my plate. It was a black sludge full of mysterious pig parts. I picked at it with my fork.

Sylvia scooped a smear of it into her mouth.

The word *nefarious* popped to mind. Does anyone use the word *nefarious*?

"On the commune," Sylvia said, "we didn't live with our parents. The kids lived in the kids' house."

The commune? Did she really say that or was I imagining it? I felt a little unhinged. I'd studied communes for years—dead communes, but communes nonetheless—so I might have been imagining that this scarred pirate woman was telling me about growing up on a commune.

"A cult, really," she said. "You know, esoteric rituals, human sacrifice, that kind of thing."

I looked down at the black sludge again. It smelled like death, but when I tasted it, I found it surprisingly light. Lemony.

"Seriously," she said. "I like the word *cult*. If you are in a cult, you are really committed, worshiping the Deity. Worshiping the good. That's all I want to do in this life. Worship the good."

I pictured some cult members sitting around a fire, but in my head they looked like characters from *Scooby-Doo*. I was still chewing the offal. It required a lot of chewing. "Isn't that what you are trying to do too? As a fact-checker?" she said. "Worship the truth? No matter what. Expose the way things are, not the way we pretend they are. Let the chips fall where they may. Isn't that your thing?"

Was that my thing? I felt pinned down like an insect. I didn't want to be told what my "thing" was, even if it was my "thing" to let the chips fall where they may, and yet the way she looked at me when she said it, with that scar and those sleeves, maybe that was my thing. Worship the truth. Worship the Deity. I was a bit queasy. I took another bite of organ meat. Fruitlands, Amos Bronson Alcott's vegan cult founded in 1843, jumped to mind. It didn't last a season.

Sylvia poured us more wine. We'd already gone through a carafe.

"Dionysus had a good cult," she said, taking a sip. "Back in ancient Greece, you had to join up if you wanted to learn how to make wine. Growing grapes and then turning them into this stuff—that was a special skill passed down from the gods. And the people who did it were mostly women and slaves. That was one of the cool things. They'd often pick leaders from the lowest rungs of society. For a lot of those people it was their only outlet. Make some wine. Get drunk. Dance. That was the best you could do."

"Worship the Deity," I said.

"Exactly," she said, and clanged her glass into mine, hard enough that a little of it splattered.

"Should we start our own wine cult?" I said.

"What do you think I brought you here for, fact-checker?" she said, and took another big sip. She flashed a mischievous smile. I watched her scar appear and disappear. I tasted the pigweed salad. It was a bittersweet combination that evoked a craggy stone wall, in France, maybe. I imagined Sylvia and I picnicking by it. She was wearing a plain nineteenth-century dress and her kerchief and puffy sleeves. Like a pirate on the prairie. The wall led to our wine commune. Maybe we had our own little country cottage.

"What did you say?"

Had I said something?

Just then a woman I hadn't met (short hair, figural tattoo on her left forearm) passed the donation hat to our table. It was an actual hat, a brown fedora, full of bills. I had no idea how much to give for the dinner. I'd already had a good deal of wine. Plus that signature cocktail. And now pork five ways was being piled in front of me. Josiah Warren came to mind, as he often did. Warren founded the Modern Times community in which goods and services were priced only by labor hours—work for work, time for time. Two hours of sign painting was sixteen pounds of corn. That didn't help me. I'd never painted a sign, and I'd never grown corn or anything, really, except maybe a jade plant, and even that had shriveled under my care. I had no sense of what kind of labor went into this food, what time was spent, and the value of water and land and sun and a pig's life. It had had a name, Siddhartha. Who had killed it? I pictured Sylvia chasing a wild boar with a bow and arrow. She was wearing her gladiator sandals and puffy sleeves. I was behind her. I threw in $87. It was all I had on me.

"What are you looking at?" she said.

I didn't know what I was looking at.

"You have that look sometimes, fact-checker. It's intense." she said. "Not in a bad way, but—"

I tried to change my face.

"—you remind me of this guy I knew once. He used to get that look. He was this very religious guy; he was in seminary school. Are you religious?"

"Religious? Like worshiping the Deity?"

"More like fasting and giving up drinking and sex and then freaking out and bingeing. He used to come around with that look," she said. "I couldn't resist it."

"Are you and Jarvis working on blight-resistant tomatoes?" I blurted. Maybe it was out of the blue.

"No way!" she said. "Jarvis and I don't really work together. He sticks to his hybrids."

"Which he grows at another location, right? In Pittstown?"

"Well, he—" she said. She took a big bite of pork belly and slowly chewed it. "I'm an heirloom girl," she said finally.

She said it—"I'm an heirloom girl"—in a way that sounded like it meant more than a preference, like she had some special power. She did have some special power.

"So what's this 'nefarious business' you mentioned to Mandeville?" I said. I couldn't help it.

She laughed out loud.

"Still fact-checking, huh? You *are* a dedicated cult member," she said. "I know it's your job. I know you don't want to say something is OK when it's not OK. You don't want to sign off on bullshit. I respect that. But, really, isn't Mandy pretty full of shit? What's the point of his article, anyway? I'm glad if it drums up a little support for farmers—we need it—but beyond that . . ."

Sylvia adjusted her kerchief. I imagined biting her scar. Sweetly biting it.

"What would you do, anyway, if I told you about some terrible crime? Because of course there are terrible things going on in farming, just like every business in this fucking country. Suppose I told you there were human traffickers or drug dealers or gangs? What would you do about it?"

Sylvia looked at me. I heard the sound of knives and forks scraping. And the music. It was definitely Smog now.

"Seriously," she said, "I'm asking. What would you do?"

I didn't answer. Smog was bellowing something about horses.

"I think you should just take whatever I said out of the article."

"I'll mention it to Mandeville," I said, "but I can't promise anything."

# Chapter 13

# NEGATIVE MAGNUS EFFECT

I'm not entirely sure how Sylvia and I ended up at my place watching baseball on TV. I didn't exactly invite her. She must have invited herself. She needed a place to crash, she had said. She wasn't going back to the farm. She was working the market the next morning, and she didn't want to stay with Agnes for some reason. I was nervous before we arrived. I lived with several roommates so there were often people hanging out or coming or going, sometimes strangers. We lived in an anonymous tenement building in a railroad apartment that was meant to be two bedrooms but that someone had carved up into four. Mine had only one tiny window that looked out to a shaft and let in no natural light. It was simple and dark, like a monastery cell. That's what Magda said when she came to visit. "Get out. You live here now, Mr. Encyclopedia?" I remember her saying. "Of course," she said. "You're like a monk. You live in a joyless little cell." At the time we were broken up. I was pretty bitter, and I felt she was being incredibly cruel. But maybe she was right. I had only sparse furniture—an old Shaker dresser and chair—and I slept on a futon on the floor, with hundreds of books around me, books that sometimes felt like windows but often felt like shackles. They weren't getting me anywhere. We slept together that night, Magda and I. It was humiliating. And not long after, she married the Fraud.

That was the last time I had brought a woman back to my apartment, and now here I was, with Sylvia watching baseball and babbling about fluid dynamics. Hideo Nomo was pitching for the Dodgers, and we'd just run a story about the physics of pitching, so I was explaining Hideo Nomo's weird windup and his signature pitch, the forkball. The article hadn't been about these things exactly, but I was extrapolating. I knew that scientists had been trying to re-create pitches like Nomo's forkball in order to understand more precisely how they work. They understood the basic physics: The forkball and other sinking pitches drop because of something called the "negative Magnus effect," a downward force created by the seams of the ball when they rotate at a particular angle. But there were still mysteries about the forces that envelop the ball, and no matter how hard they tried, no one could exactly reproduce the trajectory of a real major-league breaking ball in the lab. They tried wind tunnels; they filled rooms with smoke and lasers. They were still guessing.

Nomo went into his "tornado" windup, coiling himself up like a spring, his back turned to the batter, and then uncorking.

"You definitely can't reproduce that in the lab," Sylvia said.

"Nomo invented that motion in order to impress his dad," I said. I don't know how I knew this. It wasn't in any article I'd checked. Just in my head. "And he used to go to sleep with a ball jammed between his fingers and taped in place. That's how he perfected his grip."

I had grabbed a tennis ball out of the bin in the hall to demonstrate the forkball grip. It hurts your hand. If you get it right, it's in the dirt. If you get it wrong, a hitter will crush it. It's a thin line.

Sylvia imitated Nomo's windup perfectly and tossed the ball down the railroad hallway. It went sputtering behind the radiator. Todd Zeile belted a 2-2 forkball to left.

"They are working on new machines right now that actually can replicate the exact spin," I said.

"*You're* kind of a machine," she said. "Do you have a pulse?"

She grabbed my wrist. I flinched, unprepared. She grabbed harder, pulling me close to her. She pressed her thumb across my veins. I could feel my blood throbbing. Her scar was inches away from my nose. She reached closer, bringing her face right up to mine, breathing on my cheek. I didn't know how to act. I saw her scar again. We didn't kiss.

"You're alive," she said, and let go.

She went to retrieve the ball. I noticed her gladiator sandals clutching her ankles. She was humming something undecipherable. A lot of things jumped into my mind at random: El Greco's Christ ascending into heaven, Magdalena's eyebrows, the failure of New Harmony, the socialist commune in Indiana.

Sylvia handed me a beer. We watched the game in silence for a while. I found myself, despite my better judgment, lecturing again, this time about pitch selection and about different counts and how the pitcher and the catcher try to fool the batter and the batter tries to guess. I told her how pitchers are effective not just by having good pitches but also by disguising their pitches, like Nomo had been trying to do. If the batter can see by the motion of the windup whether the pitch is, say, a curveball, then he has the advantage. But then if you're always trying to look for signs and guess the pitch, sometimes you forget the basics. See the ball. Hit the ball. The simplest things can be the most difficult. As I said this, I thought it might sound like some weird metaphor or some coded message. People are always using baseball as a bad metaphor. It might seem as if I were saying something about guessing her intentions or about her guessing my intentions, sexual intentions.

I was now sitting close to her, maybe too close. I felt her leg through her jeans. Was I pressing against her too much? I felt like a creep on the subway who presses up against a woman when the train is crowded, a creep who fantasizes that the girl he touches is fantasizing about him too. She wants to touch, but not too much. Sylvia's leg was warm. She is touching me too, I thought. Maybe instead of worrying, I should own up to my desire, whatever that is. I should touch Sylvia if I want to touch her and what happens, happens, I thought. I looked at the TV. Milton Bradley hit a breaking ball to left field. Two runs scored: 3–3. I pulled my leg away slightly, creating the tiniest space between us, and then nervously I started to turn. But Sylvia was already pushing me back against the couch. I felt her scar on my cheek. She was kissing me.

# Chapter 14

# TRANSFORMER

When I awoke, Sylvia was gone. I found a note from her on the table, with her hair clip sitting on top of it. The note said:

*Dear Fact-Checker,*

*Sorry to leave so early, but I have to take care of some things. You were right about that. Anyway, thanks. I'll call you in a few days.*

*XO,*
*Sylvia*

*P.S. Yes! Let's do it.*

Yes! Let's do what? And what was I right about? I couldn't remember being right about anything.

I tried to figure it out as I stood on my roof drinking coffee and staring out at Lower Manhattan. I felt like a giant wave had crashed over me and I was now being pushed and pulled by its force. It was wonderful to be in this ocean, but I didn't know which way was up or how to take a breath. Yes. Let's do it.

But what? What had I missed? That feeling rose up again, the feeling I get after difficult and intimate interviews, like the call with the CIA widow the day I first read "Mandeville/Green," just nine days before, a feeling of uncertainty and regret. Sylvia had taken me to a weird supper club to eat a whole pig and drink a lot of wine, then had come back to my house, and now she was gone. My mind, as it does, replayed all my conversations with Sylvia in random bits and pieces. I had confirmed that she didn't crossbreed tomatoes (check) and that she didn't solve late blight (check). I had learned about her father and her stepfather and about the smell of the forest. I had learned about her many attempts at cooperative living and the way the back of her neck felt when I kissed it. And how easy she had made things, how natural. What was I missing? My ears were clogged. And my brain. Perhaps it was just the residual effects of the wine. Or the pork. I was hungover again. But it seemed like something more. Like I had lost something, I was lost. Or maybe I'm misremembering now, given what followed.

I looked out at the glorious, tawdry collection of glowing skyscrapers and tried to focus on the farthest ones. Then I tried to look farther out into the harbor, to train my eyes to see more. I didn't really believe in the Fat Albert Girl's idea about vision therapy. I'd done some research, of course. Vision therapy was invented in the 1870s by the optometrist Louis Émile Javal. His father and sister were both crosseyed, so, to help them, he developed a series of exercises. Ironically, Javal himself developed glaucoma and went blind. Still, his exercises proved useful; many of them still persist; more were added over time; the field grew; and by the late twentieth century, there arose a new, controversial school called behavioral vision therapy (BVT). The practitioners, and I assume Fat Albert Girl worked for one of these, claimed that many behavioral and learning disabilities in children—everything from dyslexia to poor motivation—were often misdiagnosed as psychological issues when they are actually byproducts of vision problems. Eye exercises and coordination could help improve the condition of these patients, according to BVT. Even autistic children might benefit from eye patches and ocular training, some said.

All of this sounded ridiculous to me, but who was I to say that you couldn't improve your vision, or your life, just by trying? Maybe I was just a knee-jerk conservative. I didn't know anything about how the eyes actually worked. They were famously convoluted, projecting upside-down and backward images. The brain has to do a lot to process all that data; it does a lot of projecting, and of course it could be retrained to do so differently. You didn't need to be a crank with some hunter-gatherer view of the world to think you might not know everything about how your body works, that you couldn't know everything, or understand everything, that there may be new ways of being in the world, of sensing it, of knowing it. Maybe working with eye patches or balance beams or looking out at the Williamsburg Bridge, and then looking just past it, a little farther, and then a little farther, as I was trying to do, could change everything. I thought of Sylvia's body, but even as I thought of it, her body vanished into the city around me, already a blur. If I could just go back there.

The dinner again: Sylvia stacking pieces of tomato onto her fork and then pushing the whole thing into her mouth. Her scar. The pirate sleeves. The cults. Sylvia worshiped the Deity. She worshiped the good. She kept searching for new, better alternatives, new ways of being, of living, ways that were more organic, literally organic, but also simple, natural, beautiful, which I suppose I wanted too. Everyone does. I wanted to believe that I could live more organically, maybe not farming, but somehow that I could break through the paralysis of encyclopedic doubt. With Sylvia I could. I could have faith in something unlikely; I could take a "leap of faith," as people call it. Yes. Let's do it.

But I couldn't help thinking such a leap is most often a leap into an abyss, a fall. All utopias are failures. My professors were always asking me to distill the lessons I'd gleaned from these utopian strivers. Why tell us about them? they'd say. I had no clear answer. Some of the communes I studied were, for a time, economically successful, and some made beautiful and interesting things, and some were radically feminist and abolitionist, but they were all wrongheaded. The Shakers had weird rites, and they outlawed sex. Robert Owen was a bit of a fascist. Noyes was basically a child molester. There were certainly no perfect communities; no one could accurately and ethically engineer their social world; no one could avoid the Civil War and industrial capital and the unpredictable blur of it all. Or at least, no one had. Even the Greenmarket was full of nefarious practices. What could I do about it?

I looked hard out at the bridge, the wonderful, dreadful, industrial Williamsburg Bridge. Not beautiful like the Brooklyn Bridge, it looked more like an oil derrick, or a Transformer. I didn't know much about Sylvia. She'd left a note on the table. What did it mean? "I have to take care of some things" and "You were right about that." *That.* Was she really hiding something or was I imagining it? What was she about to say about Warren when we first met? Why did she think Mandeville was a bad cook? What exactly did she mean when she said she liked me? And why had she left her hair clip on my table? If we spent more time together, if we became friends or even more than friends, if we became lovers, would she always disappear without saying goodbye? Would she always leave her hair clip behind?

That would be OK, I thought. It was a kind of promise: We will meet again.

I was wrong about that.

# PART TWO

# UNKNOWN UNKNOWNS

# Chapter 15

# THE DEFIANT ONES

I considered stopping by the farmers market right away, that Saturday morning—I assumed Sylvia must have gone to work—but I thought it might seem pushy or intrusive to follow her after she just left my apartment. If I wanted to see Sylvia again, I should play it cool, I thought. I shouldn't "overplay my hand," as they say. Seeming too eager can be the kiss of death. Not that we all have to be Arthur Fonzarelli or have some masculine code of restraint, but even sensitive, thoughtful people—even "interesting" people—respond poorly to smothering or to the quick escalation of emotion. It smacks of desperation, and desperation may signal some deeper flaw, some irreconcilable concern that will be planted at the heart of the relationship before it even begins, and will never be able to be excised. People like to be given a bit of breathing space, especially at first. They like to take things slowly, I thought, or sometimes they do. I'd just have to wait for her to call. In any case, "Mandeville/Green" wasn't going to press for at least another week. Talking to Sylvia again could wait.

She didn't call on Sunday or on Monday. But when the phone rang in my office Tuesday morning, I had a feeling it was her. It was from a restricted number. I let it ring twice before I answered. I didn't want to seem too eager.

It wasn't Sylvia. It was Tony Curtis.

I had been fact-checking a profile pegged to a new stage version of *Some Like It Hot*. I had thought he might be hard to reach, but he wasn't. I had already talked to him once and now he was calling me, as he had promised, "first thing" Tuesday. It was 7:00 a.m. on the West Coast. Perhaps, he was just bored or perhaps he was wedded to an old-fashioned idea of publicity as in *Sweet Smell of Success* with Burt Lancaster, but he was very friendly and we spent nearly an hour on the phone.

Curtis spoke with his trademark accent, the same voice he had in *Sweet Smell of Success* (which does not, if you're fact-checking, have a *The* in the title), only slightly strained with age. It seemed almost a parody of a New Yorker's accent, although Curtis hadn't lived in New York in years. He lived in Henderson, a suburb of Las Vegas. He was now married to a buxom blonde (the reporter gave me a few snapshots) who was forty-six years his junior. It was his sixth marriage. Tony Curtis and his wife had three cats, he confirmed on the phone, including a fluffy white one named Marilyn (after Marilyn Monroe) and several small dogs including Schwartz, named after Curtis himself, who was born Bernard Schwartz.

Curtis liked to tell a story; he strung one anecdote into another. Luckily, many of the same anecdotes he told me were in the article I was checking, and without much prompting he repeated them in almost identical language. "My father was Hungarian," Tony Curtis said, "a tailor in the Bronx, a sharp dresser but poor. We lived behind the shop. I spoke only Hungarian until the age of five. I still love to speak it. Sinatra always called me Bernie. He was the only one. Sinatra was so angry. I don't know why. He just carried this anger around. He scared me, but he was wonderful to me too, taught me to sing, although he didn't know it. I would just hang around, soak it up."

It was true, Tony Curtis told me that he had dated Marilyn Monroe. "For seven sweet months," he said. He told me a long story about her relationship with Billy Wilder and then another story about having dinner with her in a club, the Mocambo. "There was this birdcage right by our table with a canary. I'm looking at it, and the canary just drops dead," he said. "It was smoky in there. Maybe it suffocated, I don't know. I looked over to Marilyn, but she hadn't noticed the bird. And just like that, before I say a thing, a waiter comes by, reaches into his coat, pulls out some nylons, and snatches up the dead bird. Another waiter comes up right behind him and puts a new canary in the cage. It blew my mind. I think about that a lot, you know: Life is fragile," Tony Curtis said, "and, bam, you can just be replaced."

That story wasn't in the piece, but I didn't interrupt him. I spent the whole time wondering how I might check whether he had really said that Marilyn Monroe's "pussy tasted like champagne." I didn't really need to get him to repeat these exact words but needed to make sure he might say that kind of thing. Then I could just trust the reporter. I felt uncomfortable asking him about pussy. I didn't even like to say *pussy*. It was hard to find any words for sex that didn't seem to suggest some bad version of masculinity. Did you have intercourse? I could ask him. How were your relations? I was worried that I might sound like Mr. Lancaster talking about "motherfuckas." I wasn't very good at talking about sex or, for that matter, desire in general. I was, according to Magda, a prude. Mr. Encyclopedia, the Prude. I hoped this hadn't put Sylvia off. She seemed perfectly good at desire. *She* kissed *me* after all. And then, well, things just happened, or that's how I remember things, although I wasn't sure that's how things seemed for her. I may have been missing the signs. I had drunk a lot that night, and eaten a lot of organ meats. I didn't even understand her note to me the next morning. "Yes! Let's do it"? Tony Curtis was still talking about Marilyn Monroe. I imagined saying, "How was her pussy, Mr. Curtis? Can you describe its flavor?" He paused. I asked, "Do you remember making love to her, Tony?" That's the phrase I used in the end: *making love*.

"Do I remember it?" he said. "How can you forget a pussy like that? It was like Dom Pérignon." He made a sort of kissing noise into the phone. I wrote *Dom Pérignon* in the margin in case the reporter wanted to add that detail. "I was twenty-three when I met her," he said. "Howard Duff had this house in Malibu on the beach, he was an actor, and he gave me the keys. This was our first night together, and I tried to cook us a steak, out on the grill, right there on the beach, and a lot of sand got on the steak," Tony Curtis said. "But I pretended there wasn't any and so did she. Boy, did we fall in love."

For the most part, I didn't worry too much about whether Tony Curtis's stories were strictly true. The profile read like an oral history, and the reader would understand these to be Tony Curtis's words and would treat them with the appropriate skepticism. Tony Curtis was probably not the most reliable source, even about his own life. His claims about "pussy," even his use of the word *pussy*, were enough to suggest exaggeration or outright lies. It was clear that he had developed a self-mythology, as we all do to some extent. Of course, I checked everything that had an external reference. That's what checkers do. I had already confirmed that the Bellagio, where Curtis and his young wife liked to disco dance, had eleven original Picassos and eighty-three security cameras in one dining room, and that Curtis owned an Andy Warhol painting of an orange-yellow boot called *The Some Like It Hot Shoe*. Tony himself was an aspiring painter.

The only worrisome fact—a fact that really did have historical significance—was a claim Tony made about *The Defiant Ones*. Tony said that he had insisted that Sidney Poitier and he get equal star billing for that film and that Poitier was the first Black actor billed above the title. I had to check those things even if they appeared in a quote and were thus understood to be "according to Tony Curtis." We didn't allow people to lie or misinform our readers about anyone's achievements. They couldn't just credit themselves as civil rights pioneers, just like they couldn't blame others for wrongdoing without some evidence. Whether we were praising someone or casting aspersions, we needed corroboration. That's Fact-Checking 101.

After some searching, I found a film encyclopedia that agreed that *The Defiant Ones* was the first instance in which an African American had been billed above the title in mainstream Hollywood. (I wrote *mainstream Hollywood* in the margin.) I began looking for Sidney Poitier's contact information. I thought he'd be the best one to confirm or deny the story, but reaching him, I knew, was a long shot. I called the Screen Actors Guild. I called the Association of Talent Agents. I called the University of Southern California, where he sat on the board of the film school. No luck.

Finally I found a number for his agent in an old directory. It was a fairly unreliable source, so I didn't have high hopes. A man picked up. I told him I was trying to get in touch with Sidney Poitier. "What for?" he said. The voice was a familiar baritone. It sounded a lot like Sidney Poitier's. I stammered for a moment, then recovered my formal manner.

"I'd like to speak to Mr. Poitier regarding a story we are running that mentions the film *The Defiant Ones*," I said. "I'd like to confirm some facts about that film's production, facts that concern Mr. Poitier directly."

"What exactly would you like to know?" The deep voice rumbled across the phone line with such Poitier-like authority that I was for a moment quite intimidated and I hoped I was pronouncing "Poitier" correctly. There was something about that voice that demanded respect. Still, I wasn't entirely sure this was the real Poitier on the phone, so I didn't throw all my cards on the table. I didn't mention exactly what Tony Curtis had said.

"Well, sir, it's about the billing of the film. It's my understanding that this was the first major Hollywood feature to bill an African American actor above the title."

"That's right."

"I'd like to ask Mr. Poitier"—Pwa-tee-ay; I said it quickly—"who made that decision."

"Tony Curtis," the voice said. "He demanded it. I remember it well."

"And to whom am I speaking?" I asked.

"This is Sidney Poitier," he said. "Is the article about Tony?"

"It is."

"Tony made sure we got equal billing," the deep voice continued. "He told Stanley Kramer we had to be given the same of everything. That was Tony," he said, "a good man."

I'm not normally starstruck, but that phone call left me a bit shaken. I suppose it was the fact that I'd called a number, almost at random, and spoken to Sidney Poitier. Or perhaps it was the voice and the authoritative way he spoke. He called me "son" at one point.

I was not a particular Poitier fan. When I dated Magdalena, we had watched many of his movies on one of our film history binges. (Magda loved old movies. We would watch everything by Ernst Lubitsch, every amnesia movie, everything with Sidney Poitier, etc.) But I couldn't even think of a single one of Poitier's films that I had enjoyed. *To Sir, with Love* was sentimental and formulaic. *Guess Who's Coming to Dinner* annoyed me with its 1960s moralism, and I'd always disliked Spencer Tracy. I didn't understand what Katharine Hepburn, beautiful and nimble-minded, saw in that self-satisfied troll when someone like me would have made more sense for her. I wondered who might play me in a movie about the magazine. I imagined it as an old screwball comedy. I wanted to be Cary Grant. But I was probably more of a Ralph Bellamy, a boob who thinks he's a good guy (maybe he is) but he can't see what's going on right in front of him. And what about Sylvia? She had a bit of Hepburn to her—tall, strong-willed—but I sensed she was more of a Carole Lombard, zany, unpredictable, Carole Lombard in a movie about a spirited young pirate woman who joins a commune to hide out from her pursuers and upends everything. Carole Lombard had a scar on her face as well. Then Lombard died tragically.

Not that I was worried about Sylvia dying. Not yet anyway.

# Chapter 16

# NEW BORSCHT

I was distracted the rest of that week. It didn't help that Charles kept assigning me different tasks with quick turnarounds. I checked a short review of a restaurant that served something called "New Borscht," and then a poem with a smattering of references to quantum mechanics, and then a blurb about an upcoming concert featuring one hundred tubas, and, of course, all the while, I was tracking down odds and ends about the war. Or the wars. I didn't have much time to concentrate on "Mandeville/Green," which still had quite a lot of unchecked passages. It was weighing on me. Somewhere in the back of my mind, Sylvia's quote about the "nefarious" practices in the market was weighing on me too, especially since she had told me nothing about that—nothing that I remembered anyway. But that wasn't my main concern about Sylvia that week, the week after she had slept with me and left at dawn. Mostly I wondered if she had seen the Swedish commune movie *Together*. I had it on DVD.

But she didn't call me. Neither did her boss, Jack Jarvis. He emailed me instead. Emails are not the best ways to check facts. The respondents never answer every question, and it's hard to ask follow-up questions or assess tone and context. But Jarvis had insisted and had sent a long, annoying email that Friday. He confirmed basic claims we made about the economics of New Egypt. It was true that he'd gotten hundreds of thousands of dollars in external funding from philanthropists or the farm, which was actually a nonprofit, the Geodynamic Agricultural Institute. Also true: He'd combined his CSA with an on-site learning program. New Yorkers and suburbanites could pay for a biweekly dump of vegetables and could also work at the farm. There were lectures and meals for these "contributing members," some of whom paid a pretty penny for the title. But he didn't answer all my questions, and I couldn't easily follow up or ask about Sylvia. Instead, I had to read more of his messianic philosophy:

"Everyone," he emailed to me, "should experience the facts of growth, the fat of life. Everyone should cut their fruit from the tree and pull their life out of the earth. They should feel the scythe in their hands and sever the root. Only then can they be healthy. Only then can he be whole." Although I couldn't stand Jarvis's overblown rhetoric or his insistence on emailing me his overblown rhetoric when I was simply trying to check facts, something about what he was saying appealed to me, especially after meeting Sylvia. I knew that factory farming was terrible. I thought that we should all know the origins of our food. I did want to restore my connection to the earth. I did want to regrow my roots. Maybe Sylvia could help me.

But what about my other questions? Were *most* (this was a key word) of his workers "students" or "interns," who were given room and board and a small stipend for two years while they worked with "masters," most of whom visited occasionally to give lectures and demonstrations? The whole strange amalgam of entrepreneurship, volunteerism, and "education" at New Egypt seemed exploitative to me—exploitation reimagined as a pastoral ideal, like some capitalist commune. He had "synergized" with partners to revolutionize our growing practices. Laborers be damned. What did Sylvia think of this?

I found myself staring up at the ceiling. I did this sometimes, especially when I was stuck on something. I'd been doing it ever since 9/11, or actually just after 9/11, when I checked a story about the reasons for the collapse of the World Trade Center. I had interviewed a demolition expert who told me about the floor joists, the things that ultimately burned and buckled. The floor joists, he said, were weak points. Modern skyscrapers were just exterior walls with structural tubes in the middle. They didn't have big weight-bearing columns distributed throughout. They have open space—so much open space, he said. Open space is the name of the game, he told me, but that meant that the whole thing was held together by floor joists.

"Take a look," he kept saying. He was a funny guy, the demolitions expert, a stereotypical Jersey guy. Even though I realize this is a stupid classist stereotype and I myself am from suburban New Jersey, I still imagined him with slicked-back hair, a gold chain around his neck, and a host of tattoos.

"There ain't much to 'em," he said of those critical floor joists. "Take a look yourself. You gotta. Aren't ya curious? Come on, dude. Get up on your desk."

"Now?"

"Why not? I bet you can pop out a panel or two, easy. Check out what you're standing on, what holds you up there in the sky."

I got up on my desk and pushed up until the ceiling panel above me gave way. I stuck my head into the crawl space.

"You're right," I said, "there ain't much to them." I said *ain't* for effect, but immediately felt odd about it. And besides, I didn't know if he was right. I couldn't see much up there in the dark. There were some ducts and some wires. Mostly it was a vast, dark space, a space I'd rather not consider.

I was looking up at the ceiling, thinking about how strange it is to stand inside a giant building held up so high in the air, with other people standing inside a giant building on other floors, each in their own world, and how hard it is, at any minute, to know exactly where you are and what caused you to be there, and what you should do next. I was thinking about Sylvia and the things she said about worshiping the Deity, and about the way her body felt, and about the dead canary in Tony Curtis's story, and about vision therapy and the Fat Albert Girl, and how anyone can live a good life, an honorable life, an organic life, a life that will make things better, both day to day and in general, for oneself and for others. In other words, I was thinking about the things we all think about all the time while we wait for a potential lover or a fact-checking source to call us when they said they would call "in a few days" and six days had passed, and they haven't called.

I looked at my phone. It didn't ring.

# Chapter 17

# THE UN-AMERICANS

I went to Union Square the next day. I had decided to find Sylvia, but when I got there, I hesitated. I circled around the market for a while without approaching New Egypt. I don't know why. Maybe I still wanted to play it cool, like Fonzie. I'm pretty sure that a week after a woman begins to tell you about some enigmatic problem she has at work, then invites herself over to your house, sleeps with you, and disappears, leaving her hair clip and a note saying "Yes! Let's do it," it's perfectly reasonable to ask after her. But when she doesn't have a cell phone and you go to her workplace and just wander around aimlessly looking at the people and wondering what secrets they might be harboring, what ideals they might hold dear, what alternative lives they might imagine, and what nefarious practices they may partake in, as I did that Saturday morning, it feels weird.

I ended up talking with a young blonde woman who just started working at the Council on the Environment of New York City. She was on her gap year, she said. I imagined a gap year as a huge break in the space-time continuum. I tried to explain this to her, but it didn't take. I didn't really know what I was talking about. Then I found a bench on the north side of the square with a good view of New Egypt. I took alternate sips of a sugared-up iced coffee I'd gotten from the better of the two corner bodegas on Broadway, and a blackberry yogurt drink from Ronnybrook Farms. I watched the shoppers wandering to and fro. I looked out at Barnes & Noble. I gazed up Park Avenue South. I looked as far as I could and then a bit farther. Maybe farther. I didn't see Sylvia. I didn't see anyone engaging in any "nefarious" activities, or if I did, I didn't recognize them. How would I?

I finally approached New Egypt.

"Looking for Sylvia?" Nick asked before I could say anything. It felt like an accusation.

"She hasn't been around," he said. "I'm not sure what happened to her." Nick stepped close to me and spoke softly. It seemed everyone involved with "Mandeville/Green" was doing this to me, confiding in me, yet I felt no one was really telling me anything.

"I heard she skipped town," Nick said.

*Skipped town?* I thought. Who uses that expression? Don't you have to have bookies after you, or the law or at least a mad and jealous lover, in order to "skip town"? I certainly wasn't a jealous lover. Or I didn't think I was.

"I heard she went to Mexico," Nick said. "I don't know. I was a little worried about her, but you know Sylvia."

I nodded blankly. I didn't know Sylvia. Not really. A tan middle-aged woman who was shopping for tomatoes squeezed by me. The yoga mat that was strapped to her back struck me on the side of the head. (I silently checked off some of Mandeville's descriptions of Greenmarket shoppers.) She reached for some tomatoes right in front of me. "Excuse me," she said. I smiled and sorted through some Ramapos, trying to detect their ripeness. I looked for small, irregular shapes. Irregular-looking fruit, I thought, seemed more authentic and therefore more delicious, although I realized this was probably erroneous logic. I picked up one and sniffed it. I couldn't smell it, though. Her armpit was close to me, and I could only smell the woman. She smelled of lavender and something slightly sour.

"You don't have a phone number for her?" I asked Nick. "Or an email or anything?"

"No, dude, she doesn't have a cell phone. She's like the only one left who uses pay phones." He blew into his cheeks, joke-exasperated. "She hasn't been at the farm this week. She was supposed to be working the market, but I don't know. Jack put me in charge."

"No one has heard from her?"

He shrugged.

"Maybe you should ask Jack. He seemed to know she wouldn't be around." He picked a rotting tomato off the table. "I think she had some beef with him," he said, "but don't quote me on that." He laughed nervously, perhaps realizing I might quote him.

"Have you tried those?" Nick asked me. I looked down and realized I was fondling a tomato. It was a wine-black heirloom called a Paul Robeson.

"They're pretty great," Nick said. "The Robesons."

"Yes, they're wonderful," said the yoga lady.

Nick began to cut one up for us to sample.

"They're Russian," I said. "Paul Robesons." This had been mentioned in Mandeville's piece. I now knew a lot about tomato varieties.

Nick held one up and began a rendition of "Ol' Man River." The yoga lady looked confused.

"You know. Paul Robeson was that singer with the deep voice."

"Oh, of course," the yoga woman said. "He's won-der-ful."

"Robeson was big in Russia?" Nick asked.

"He was a leftist," I said. "The Russians loved him. Some say he was a sympathizer."

"So you think the tomato is like a tribute?" Nick asked me as I reached for a slice. "Like for the American comrade?"

"He never admitted to being a communist," I said. "But he visited Russia. The FBI had a file on him." I popped the purple tomato into my mouth.

"The FBI probably has a fucking file on me; it doesn't mean I'm a goddamn communist," Nick said, suddenly shouting. The FBI probably did have a file on him, I thought. *I* had a file on him. I'd already dug up his arrest record: possession of marijuana, unlawful assembly, resisting arrest. "It's not like that's your only choice: You're either in favor of the American racist imperialist military-industrial complex or you're a communist." Nick was trying to sound calm and enlightened in front of the yoga woman, not like a raving lunatic. It wasn't working. "Everyone is always trying to label you," he said, spitting.

"How much are they?" the woman who smelled of lavender asked. We both turned to her. "The commie tomatoes," she said.

Nick sold her some Robesons while I put another slice in my mouth and let it dissolve on my tongue. Paul Robeson, the son of a slave, who won a scholarship to Rutgers, became valedictorian, went on to Columbia Law School, played in the NFL, became an acclaimed Shakespearean actor, supported the Republicans in the Spanish Civil War, marched with labor unions and African freedom fighters, was blacklisted, had his passport revoked, told the House Un-American Activities Committee, "You are the un-Americans, and you ought to be ashamed of yourselves," and supported Stalin. Maybe he supported

Stalin. Probably. What did his tomato taste like? It was pretty good. A little too acidic.

"Nick, have you seen anything suspicious going on at the market?" I asked. The yoga woman had moved on.

"Suspicious?"

"Yeah, anything that might have bothered Sylvia? She mentioned that there was some weird stuff going on."

Nick shrugged. "There's always weird shit going on, dude. Look around." I did. I saw Warren over by the truck, glaring at a couple who were frantically squeezing zucchini. There was something weird about Warren. "Did you see the artichokes at Norwich?" Nick asked. "That's some weird shit, dude."

"Yes," I said. They had tiny purple artichokes at the Norwich stand. They were beautiful.

"Look," Nick said, "the shit people grow, man, is weird shit, amazing shit, dude. Most of them are weird folks. Freak folk, you know? And a lot of them grow excellent food. So much food comes through here four days a week, direct from the ground to all these city folks in their overpriced shit-boxes. It's a fucking excellent institution if I do say so myself, and I don't fucking like institutions."

I nodded, taking another piece of tomato.

"Sylvia loves the market, dude. She loves talking to people, spreading the message. I don't think anything here spooked her. I thought it was, like, more personal. I mean, if something—"

"Personal? With Jarvis?"

"I don't know man," Nick said. "I have no fucking idea. She's probably gone on a walkabout, tired of farming. Fuck if I know."

Nick started toward the truck and then turned back to me.

"Have you talked to McDonough?" Nick asked, referring to Mac McDonough, who coordinated the Union Square Greenmarket for the Council on the Environment of New York City. "That dude knows everything that's going on."

He picked up another crate and turned toward the truck.

"He and I are going for a bite later," Nick said and walked away. I wasn't sure if it was an invitation or a statement of fact, but I thought I'd take it for the former. I pretended to look at summer squash.

# Chapter 18

# THE MANNED SEA TRADE

St. Dymphna's was a dark Irish pub with roughly hewn wooden tables. I imagined it might be a place for Dungeons & Dragons fans or those people who like to pretend-swordfight in Union Square to come and plot their medieval quest over a flagon of ale and a shepherd's pie. But I didn't see any of those people in the bar, and even though I'd ordered the shepherd's pie, Nick, McDonough, and I weren't talking about dragons or goblins; we were talking about the war in Iraq. Or Nick was. He was lecturing about how misguided the government was and how war was always a pretext for the consolidation of power. The civilian departments of the federal government, he said, were expanded much more dramatically during World War II than they were during the New Deal. War is big government.

"What's your magazine doing about it?" Nick asked me. "Your man Asprilla isn't putting up much of a fight," he said, referring to our editor in chief, Jacob Asprilla. "He's just toeing the party line, arguing about *how* Bush should be waging fucking war, not how it's all a fucking fuck-show. He's a toady."

"Nick's a libertarian," said McDonough. "Means he doesn't believe in shit. He's into Ayn Rand."

"Fuck Ayn Rand," said Nick, "and fuck you."

I looked at McDonough. He didn't react. He was a tall, ropy guy, prematurely balding. He looked like a rock climber or a cyclist.

"You must see some crazy shit at the market?" I asked.

"Crazy shit?" McDonough said. He and Nick exchanged a look. I couldn't read it.

"You know that guy Sanders?" McDonough said. "He's the guy who runs Shady Grove. He's got that braided ponytail down to his ass, like Willie Nelson."

"He grows excellent greens, all kinds of weird stuff no one grows," said Nick. "His farm is like an institution."

"He's a purist," McDonough said, "always going off on the Greenmarket for allowing pesticides and whatnot."

"Organic," said Nick, imitating a cranky old man. "We never called it that. We just called it farming. Of course it's fucking organic."

"Yeah, that's him," said McDonough. I nodded. I knew the guy by sight, although I hadn't interviewed him.

"Anyway," said McDonough. "This one morning, it was a Wednesday. I was at Union Square early before set-up, to look over two sites that we needed to change. It was, like, before sunrise when I got there, before the vendors are supposed to be there. But there was a truck parked by Sanders's spot. I was pissed. I'd been dealing with a bunch of complaints. I walked up to it, and I hear some noises inside. The liftgate was ajar, and I was ready to lay into Sanders for parking there. He knows he's not supposed to. So I open the gate. The first thing I see is this ass, this old white ass and his ponytail hanging down. Then I see this woman on her knees, her head bobbing back and forth. Dude was getting a blow job in the middle of the fucking truck. It was nasty. The girl was definitely a hooker," McDonough said, "a skinny strung-out hooker."

"Nasty," Nick said, laughing nervously.

"Sanders is moaning like a goddamn animal," McDonough continued, "and I swear I heard him say, 'Take that bitch, take that.' Right as I was opening the door: 'That'll teach you, bitch, that'll teach you.' But it, like, didn't even compute in my brain, you know; sometimes you hear see something, and it takes a minute, like: Was that real? Did I really hear see that? Then you realize you did." McDonough took a drink. "The worst part is: produce grosses me out now," he said. "I can't eat that shit now."

"And that's good shit," said Nick, throwing a French fry into his mouth.

"Fucking excellent shit," said McDonough. We all ate silently for a moment, thinking about excellent shit. And terrible shit. Exploitation. Cruelty. Magda popped to mind. If she were here, she would be angry about the way these men joked. And she would be angry at me. Or maybe she wouldn't. I don't know how she would react to an anecdote about a prostitute in a produce truck. And what about Sylvia? She always had something to say.

"Are there a lot of prostitutes around the market?" I asked.

McDonough looked at me like I was an idiot. "There's fucking fucking everywhere, isn't there? All kinds of fucking."

"Dude," said Nick, "have you ever been over to Eleventh Avenue, like, around the thirties, real early in the morning? Sometimes I drive in that way at, like, five or six o'clock; it's just crawling with hookers. I guess they're all walking home at that time. They're all wearing fishnets and ridiculous hooker outfits, even in the winter. I'm telling you. They're all half-naked."

"That's near the Javits Center," I said.

"It's also close to the docks," said McDonough.

"You think sailors are still a big part of the sex trade?" Nick asked. "Like, they are all blue balls out on the sea and when they get to port, they just need to fuck?"

The conversation went on this way, touching on the relationship between prostitution and the merchant marine, now barely existent, and about whether the demise of the manned sea trade had put pimps and call girls out of work, and, if so, where were these girls going at 6:00 in the morning on Eleventh Avenue, if they were headed home, what was their commute like, and how sad. I mentioned that there were guidebooks to New York City brothels in the early nineteenth century, describing which ones were clean and proper, and that many of those brothels were very close to Union Square and were run by women. Nick wondered if the prostitutes still had pimps, and how did the pimps dress? How might pimp fashion have evolved since the nineteenth century? We were no longer talking about nefarious practices at the market or about Sylvia, where she may have gone, and what she could have been so worried about. It wasn't prostitution, was it? Could that have been what freaked her out? I tried to turn the conversation back to the market and to ask McDonough if he had seen Sylvia or knew where she went, but just when I was about to get there, McDonough got up to leave. He had to go. He hadn't realized the time.

"I'm outta here too," said Nick.

"There must be some other shady stuff going on at the market," I said to McDonough as he grabbed his bag. "Right?"

"Man, I can tell you some stories," he said. Deadpan eyes.

"I've heard there's, like, a black market," I said, but he didn't reply. He and Nick were already heading out the door. I was about to get up and follow them, maybe to ask something else about Sylvia, but the big wooden door was closing. The sliver of bright light narrowed and disappeared.

I was left alone in the dark medieval hall. It was quiet. Everyone seemed to be drinking their own beer and thinking their own thoughts. So I worked on mine. I tried to figure out why Sylvia might have "skipped town," if she had "skipped town," and whether it had anything to do with "Mandeville/Green" or with prostitution or with terrible men or with me, not that she would skip town on my account. Somehow I felt implicated. Was that the word? *Implicated?* I had no clue what had spooked her and what she meant by "nefarious business" at the market. If it was prostitution, how did that affect her? Were farmers involved? Was it some kind of ring? Was she trying to help the prostitutes? Should I be trying to help them, as a man, or as a person? Was I implicated? I had barely touched my shepherd's pie, and now I looked down at it, a mix of lamb and mashed potatoes and brown stuff. I wondered whether shepherds actually ate shepherd's pie. Was it strange or ceremonial or just normal to eat your own sheep, ground and mashed up like this? I had no real idea what it was like to farm or to raise your own food and then to eat it. This seemed like a terrible mistake on my part, to be a human so alienated from his own food, to be a meat eater who'd never killed anything. Although that would soon change.

What kind of life was I living? Jarvis was probably right: I was living in a corridor of doom. I had to regrow my roots. Maybe I should join the homesteaders that Mandeville was profiling for his next piece. They ate only what they grew or killed. An image popped into my head: a label I'd seen on a cheese, a tiny wheel of cheese, like the kind you get on an airplane. It showed a cow sitting down and eating cheese. This image often came back to me, a cow eating cow's-milk cheese, maybe cheese made from her own milk. Weird. It had only been a week since Sylvia left her hair clip on my table on top of the note that said that she was going to "take care of some things." She might have meant anything—something personal, probably: another man, or a coworker, or the crops themselves. Perhaps climate change or some disease was the threat. I ordered another Smithwick's and looked up at the image of Saint Dymphna over the bar. I tried not to think about Saint Dymphna, an Irish teenager whose father raped her, then chased her halfway across Europe, and then killed her. Now she was a patron saint for the nervous, the emotionally disturbed, the mentally ill, and this establishment. I ate some more shepherd's pie. It was good but mushy. I couldn't tell what was what.

# Chapter 19

# A FISH

Even though I loved watching baseball, I hated playing it when I was young, hated it. My parents dropped me off at Little League again and again. I still have this sense memory of walking from the car down a hill of wet grass across the lonely field by the quarry. We didn't always practice there, but that field really sticks in my mind, and that image still fills me with dread. I never seemed to know the other kids on my team, even if I played with them for years. They seemed bigger and more aggressive than the kids from my school, although this was probably just a false impression. I was afraid of the ball. Or maybe it's better to say I was afraid of dropping the ball in front of people. The coaches stuck me out in right field, as they did to the worst fielders, and I would stand there and hope that the ball never came my way. I didn't want to have to "get under it." I rarely caught even a routine pop-up. In fact, the more routine the pop-up, the more difficult I found it. There was that painful slow time when the ball arced through the air. It was excruciating. Was I under it? Yes. No. Yes. No. Too late. These pop-ups were rare, but I spent all the rest of the time, the hours of downtime between pitches, fearing them. I hated this nothing time too. Nothing was always a potential of something, a potential of failure. In this way baseball was a lot like fact-checking: The potential of failure is always there. As a kid, I cried after practice. Eventually my parents let me quit.

Despite all this, I'd been playing on the magazine's softball team for some time. To call it a "team" was perhaps overstating it. It was more of a gathering. There was a series of scheduled games against other magazines and media outlets in Central Park. Whoever showed up for the games played, and afterward we all went for beer and pizza at a bar called Lo Life. The whole thing was low-pressure. Many of the players had never donned a glove, and we weren't very good. A lot of the younger assistants and most of my friends played. So I did too.

That Tuesday night, ten days after Sylvia had left my apartment at dawn and three days after I heard that she had "skipped town," we played *High Times*, the marijuana magazine. *High Times* was always a big game. Although some of their players supposedly did bong hits before the games, they were one of the most serious teams. They were much more serious than we were. Their shortstop wore two batting gloves and compression leggings. Their center fielder put eye-black under his eyes. Many of my teammates loved to mock their competitiveness. It reaffirmed our superiority as a "real" magazine with the class, and I use that word pointedly, not to care too much about softball. I thought it was funny, but I didn't dwell. I still had a lingering dread of the outfield.

I was in right center in the fourth when a ball was hit my way, a routine pop-up. The feeling came back. Baseball is hard. I read somewhere that major-league outfielders judge the ball mostly by sound. They are attuned to the crack of the bat and some internal sense of physics takes over, calculating speed and arc and trajectory. Some hitters at the old Shea Stadium, I'd heard, liked to hit when a plane was flying overhead from nearby LaGuardia Airport. It would disrupt the fielders' sense of hearing and give the hitters a better chance. I thought at first that the ball was hit in front of me, but as I jogged in, I realized I'd miscalculated. I backpedaled. I looked up at the dirty white blur against the wine-dark twilight. I sped up.

Baseball was popular in the Oneida utopian community in the nineteenth century. They would sometimes stop work in the middle of the day for a game. They believed, following French philosopher Charles Fourier, that you should alternate between physical and mental labor, spending no more than two hours on a task before moving to something different. They also believed in switching sexual partners regularly as a way of avoiding selfishness. No one should be committed to a single other person; they should be committed to the whole community. There was something to this idea, I thought, although I knew that church leaders like John Humphrey Noyes got their pick of the women, and I knew I wouldn't like this partner switching if I were in Oneida. I would feel betrayed, like I did by Magda, or get fixated, like I was now on Sylvia.

I stopped under the ball, still falling through the dusk. I thought I had misjudged it again, but when I reached up, I felt a soft thud. I had it. One out.

At the bar I played pool with Elizabeth and Mike. We bought each other whiskey and discussed our favorite bars in the world. Elizabeth's was on the seaside in Whitstable, a place called Hope and Anchor. It was dark and covered in crustaceans, and it served excellent local bitter and scampi and chips. Mike liked a place in Shreveport where they played live zydeco music every night. I mentioned a place in New Haven where Magda and I used to go, a dive bar called Rusty's. What made it great? Elizabeth asked.

I struggled to describe it. I was in bars all the time, almost every day, but I had little to say about them. If you want to know about water, don't ask a fish. "Nothing," I said. "I don't know. The food was bad. The jukebox was terrible. It was ugly. Plus, sometimes it would just be closed."

"That sounds fucking terrible," said Mike.

"Yeah," I said. "It was, but somehow I liked it." It's hard to know why you're drawn to things sometimes. I knew what drew me to Magdalena initially—she was smart and beautiful and full of a strange magnetic energy—but there was always something inaccessible about her. She was trouble, absent trouble now, absent trouble best forgotten. I didn't know what I thought of Sylvia, not really, but I still had some lingering feeling surrounding her, something like dread mixed with desire, a fish, a fear and a wish. It was wrapped up in a lot of things, including her scar and her cults and her secret fears about the Greenmarket story and my concerns about her weird New Age corporate boss and prostitution in the park and the way she fed me tomatoes and leaned over me, and was she in trouble? And she was kissing me, and it was wonderful. I couldn't untangle my desires and fears, my ideals and my suspicions. She was a source for a minor story who may have "skipped town," maybe to Mexico. I didn't really *need* to talk to her again. The story could go to press without her, and life would go on. That I knew.

Elizabeth was racking the balls at that point. I had control of the table. I was pretty good at pool. Or I was good enough to win a few games on a small table in a small bar against drunk people. You didn't have to make great shots or clear the table on your first turn to do that. You just had to stifle your opponent. You needed to control the cue ball so that if you missed, your opponent was left in a bad position.

Drunk players aren't usually good enough to deal with bad positions. They hit the ball hard and knock everything around and open things up for you. Elizabeth was good at pool—better than me. She had a better eye. But, for whatever reason, I usually beat her. I knocked two in off the break, solids, and lined up my next shot, the four in the corner. Pool always makes me think of Magdalena's husband, my old professor, Frank the Fraud. He believed everything in history lined up like pool shots, four ball in the corner. Aim and shoot. He hated any "theory" that might mess with his billiard ball thinking. I sunk the ball but lost the game.

Nelson put "The Night They Drove Old Dixie Down" on the jukebox, and he and Elizabeth sang along. I mumbled along too, unsure of the words but pretending. Then they played it again. I added some Willie Nelson. A guy from *High Times* bought me a whiskey. I told him about Oneida, the baseball-playing commune of free love Christians who believed they could live perfect lives on earth, partly through eugenics, but then gave up the pursuit and started a silver-ware company. He told me the plot of the novel he was writing. It was about the president's daughter who was a high-class call girl. A young Secret Service officer was sent to protect her. The *High Times* guy went into great detail. I forget the fine points, but I remember that Willie Nelson sang "Good Hearted Woman" while he was talk-ing and that in the end the G-man had to choose between his love of the president's profligate daughter and his love of the country. I fell asleep in the subway on the way home.

# Chapter 20

# BLOOD AND
# SHRAPNEL EVERYWHERE

I wasn't sure how to get into the office building on Pearl Street. It had taken me a while to find it. I kept tracking back to Exchange Place. Finally, I was able to retrace my steps with Sylvia. I found the loading dock, but I didn't have the key. I made my way around to the front of the building. The façade was lined with classical columns, each topped by stern-looking figures in rigid concrete togas. I found the front door and peered into a small marble lobby where an aged doorman was sitting. He looked on the verge of sleep or some even more deeply catatonic state. I stood frozen outside the door. I tried to remember what floor the Heads and Tails Supper Club was on. The seventh? I didn't know what to say to the doorman. What was I doing there in the first place?

A few years before we used to get these messages on our apartment answering machine from this guy Leon who had a crush on one of my roommates, a woman named Christine. She wasn't interested. Still, he left messages for all of us. One night, he called several times from the Mexican bar and restaurant around the corner. We were all at home, I seem to remember, but no one bothered to pick up. In the last message, Leon said, trying to sound excited, "Things are just getting heated up over here." This became a catchphrase for me and my roommates then. I thought about Leon as I entered the building on Pearl Street that Wednesday evening to try to find a woman whom I barely knew but about whom I was unnaturally worried. Things are just getting heated up over here, I said to myself. I headed straight for the elevator. I thought that if I looked confident and cool, like I knew exactly where I was going, the doorman wouldn't stop me. But confident and cool is not my forte.

"Can I help you?" he asked.

"Um, yes, I'm looking, I'm going, I think it's the seventh floor." He looked at me blankly. "I'm looking for a woman," I said, "Agnes, uh—Murray—she, um, works here," I said. "Red hair. Tall. Agnes?"

"Is she expecting you?" the doorman asked. He had a lisping accent. I guessed Cuban.

"Well, yes, sir," I said.

"She's not here," he said. I blinked a few times, confused by the order of his questions.

"She's not?" I said. "Agnes Murray?"

"No," he said. I stood there for a moment.

"Uh, do you know when she'll be in?"

"After work," he said.

I looked at my watch. It was almost 7:00. "After work?" I asked. He just nodded. He wasn't offering anything else. No one seemed to have any clear answers for me these days. I left.

I looked again at the ugly façade of the building and then up at the Woolworth Building, once the tallest in the world, now something like an old castle, a remnant of another era. I went back inside.

"Are any of Agnes's officemates in?" I asked. "It's kind of important."

He shrugged. "I just know Agnes," he said. He smiled. The smile didn't seem like it was meant for me.

"Well, do you know where she is?"

He yawned. The yawn lasted awhile.

"Moran's," he said finally. "Wednesday she's at Moran's." He opened his mouth and looked like he was going to say something else, but he didn't. He just yawned again.


Moran's was a faux Irish pub in the Battery Park City development, which itself had the feel of a giant corporate theme park. It catered to young Wall Street types who lived in the residential towers or commuted from Jersey. It was right on the Hudson, with outdoor seating near a garden of wildflowers and thistles. I thought how nice it could be and how nice it wasn't. The New York waterfront was either blighted or, like this area, soulless. That night it seemed like a manicured ghost town.

Agnes was wearing a ridiculous green vest and tie, like a croupier at an Irish-themed casino, but somehow she made it look hip—the tie, loosened and askew, her hair in a wild red swirl—and sexy—the vest cinching her breast and her waist. I had been at the bar a few minutes before she noticed me, but when she did, she made a show of it.

"Hey there, magazine man," she said. "What are you doing down here? Working on an article about early man?" She nodded toward the young crew-cutted men on the other side of the horseshoe bar. They were chugging beers. One yelled, "Don't be a pussy, pussy." Agnes raised her eyebrows.

"I'll have what they're having," I said.

"Irish car bombs," she said. An image popped into my head, a photo I'd seen of a market in Afghanistan, torn apart, blood and shrapnel everywhere. Calcium ammonium nitrate.

"What's an Irish car bomb?" I asked.

"You drop a shot of Jameson in a Guinness," Agnes said. "Try one?"

Before I responded, Agnes shouted across the bar, "Hey, guys, this gentleman over here says he can down a car bomb quicker than any of you. Any takers?" I looked at her dumbly. Oh God. Car bomb wars with America's finest.

One of the guys, a Dennis the Menace in a starched white shirt, said, "Fuck, yeah, dude. You're on." I smiled an unthreatening smile. He whispered something to his friend, and they giggled. Agnes poured the drinks. She poured one for herself too.

"I'm off in ten minutes," she whispered. "Bottom's up," she shouted at the boys. I drank quickly. I downed half of it in a few gulps and the rest in one. I saw the two men, or boys, starting to dribble beer down their shirts. I saw Agnes gulping hers. I put my glass down. Agnes did the same. Hers was two-thirds full. Mine, empty. The crew-cut boys kept going. They both slammed theirs down.

"I won," yelled the Menace. "Fuck you did," said the other guy. They both looked at me. Nasty drunk leers.

"Now, boys," Agnes said, "play nice." She moved over to them, defusing the tension.

"You're a good sport," Agnes said when she returned with a fresh beer for me. She put her hands on the bar in front of me and leaned in. "Now, what are you really doing here?" she asked in a way that suggested she knew the answer, or she didn't really care. Her lips were painted dark crimson, like Magda's. "Are you gonna put me in your magazine?" she said.

"I'm looking for Sylvia," I said.

"Sylvia?" she said. "I thought she was with you."

With me?

"Well, if she's not with you, she's probably out in the country somewhere, maybe shacked up with some other dude. She's always off on some crusade, and there's always someone looking for her," Agnes said. I drank a sip of beer to wash away the other, tainted beer. "She's nuts." She twirled her finger near her temple to indicate Sylvia's craziness. "I told her, I think she gets a little shack-simple out there on that farm. And I don't trust that Jack guy."

"Jack Jarvis?"

"Is that his name? The farm guy. He's got that jailbait girlfriend and all those little hippies kissing his ass. It's pretty skeezy if you ask me."

"You met him?"

"Yeah, I went out there once. And Sylvia talks about him. I don't think she likes him either, but you know Sylvia." Why was everyone saying "you know Sylvia"? I didn't know Sylvia. Did they know Sylvia? What would "knowing" her even mean?

Agnes went over to help a group of girls with ironed hair. They ordered a bucket of Coronas.

"Hey," she said when she returned. "I'm off now. Wanna buy a girl some dinner?" She gave me a half smile, half glare that made me want to do what she said and also made me doubt myself. I looked at her tight green vest. "Don't worry about Sylvia," Agnes said. "You've got a real woman right here." She grabbed my hand. "Live flesh and blood," she said. She let out an ironic laugh.

I suddenly thought of Magda. Before I left graduate school, I would walk her dog every day. I was pretty sure she was sleeping with Frank at that point. In any case, she wasn't sleeping with me. Not that it was entirely her fault. But it wasn't entirely my fault either.

# Chapter 21

# THE AMERICAN VENUS

Agnes and I took a slight detour on the way to dinner in order to check out the Irish Hunger Memorial. I'd read about it in "Johnson/Memorials," and I knew it was a stone's throw from Moran's. Agnes said she could lead me there. She'd been there a few times before. She liked the view from the top.

"But I wouldn't have even noticed it if it wasn't for Sylvia."

Sylvia?

"Blight," Agnes said. "She had this whole thing about blight. That's what started the potato famine. It killed some of Sylvia's tomatoes too."

Yes. Late blight. *Phytophthora infestans*.

It didn't look like a memorial; it didn't look like anything recognizable. It was a giant wedge of stones and grasses cantilevered over the Hudson River walkway like some kind of sprouting spaceship. I followed Agnes inside, although there wasn't really an "inside," just a hallway filled with quotes about famine etched into slick, modern walls. We walked up the path and out to a grassy area where there were low, rough stone walls like you'd find in the Irish countryside. The path looped among gorse and foxgloves and various lichens. I didn't realize it at the time, but the architects had planted native Irish flora and had brought in stones from each of the counties of Ireland. They even airlifted a ruined cottage from County Mayo and staged it on the platform; they had created a fallow potato field. Packed into this little walkway on top of the stone spaceship, among the barren glass towers of Lower Manhattan, were the greatest hits of the Irish countryside. It reminded me of a Marcel Duchamp installation in the Philadelphia Museum of Art: Hidden in a darkened corner gallery is a giant slatted wooden door with two eyeholes. Peering through them, you see a rural scene: a waterfall and a naked woman lay in the distance. Possibly a rape scene. Or a murder.

Agnes was at the top of the path looking out at the Hudson. The sun was setting, but the air was still leaden, and I felt myself sweating through my undershirt. I always wear a collared shirt, an undershirt, and long pants, no matter how hot it gets. Agnes, who had changed into a vintage yellow sundress, looked bright and cheerful. She liked to take in the view and think about being famous.

"At first I felt weird about it," she said. "I'm three-quarters Irish, you know, so I felt like I should be contemplating the famine when I came up here, not fame. I should get sad about all these dead people and hate the British. But I don't feel much connection to this whole—" She gestured back to the mini-Ireland behind us.

"I grew up in the suburbs," she said. "This whole thing seems unreal, you know? Like a TV show or something. I was kind of surprised that you wanted to come here. It's not like something people do—but then, I guess you *would* be interested in this. You and Sylvia."

Me and Sylvia. We were both something, but what? I looked at the ersatz Ireland behind me again. It was a beautiful place, despite everything. Not just beautiful, though. I pictured Sylvia here in her pirate sleeves and I kept thinking, despite my better judgment, that there was some clue to her whereabouts here. She had brought Agnes to this fake Ireland like she had taken me to Charlotte Temple's grave, a fake memorial, where she had told me that people always care about the wrong things. She must have been telling me something about the right things to care about, about the things that she cared about, about the things she had to "take care of" on the morning she left my apartment and disappeared without another word.

What was the point of the Hunger Memorial? Why re-create the countryside that had starved these people? What does it say about our relationship to food and nature? And why here in the Financial District among all these signs of financial opulence and waste? Why now? It was only a few years old, built just after 9/11, less than half a mile from Ground Zero, and it was already a forgotten thing. That I could see. The Wall Streeters were not coming up here to rethink their greed and sell off their Monsanto holdings. Almost no one knew that this memorial existed or why it did, like the grave of Charlotte Temple, which had once inspired misdirected tears. Someday the 9/11 memorial would fade away too.

When I was researching "Johnson/Memorials," I learned that there was a *Titanic* memorial in a park I used to walk through every day. I'd never even noticed. It just blended into the city. I finally looked at it, only because I had read about it. It is centered around a life-size bronze figure, a woman on a bed. She seems to be resting, but her face does not look peaceful, and one of her legs is hanging over the side of the concrete plinth as if she might be falling off. The model for that statue, I learned, was a woman named Audrey Munson. She was famous in the twenties, nicknamed the "American Venus." You can still see her all over New York. She became the model for *Civic Fame* atop the Municipal Building and *Duty* and *Sacrifice* at the Firemen's Memorial, and the *Spirit of Industry* on the Manhattan Bridge. She once wrote a series of articles for the *New York American* criticizing standards of beauty and advocating for women's rights. Later her landlord fell in love with her and murdered his wife and then killed himself in prison. Audrey Munson spent her last sixty-five years in a mental hospital. Audrey Munson, now forgotten. In Straus Park, where I used to walk, she was supposed to represent Memory itself, memory fading into the background, memory dangling off the bed. Now no one remembers her.

Perhaps Sylvia told me that night, the night we spent together, what she needed to "take care of" and what taking care of it might mean besides visiting memorials or making sure you size a woman's rug properly after her husband dies in Afghanistan or that you confirm something really "nefarious" is going on in Union Square, just so you can check off a sentence and send it off into the world to disappear like everything else. But if she did tell me, or even drop a hint, I couldn't remember it. And there was nothing in the memorials to tell me where she was; she wasn't dropping clues. That was ridiculous. Sylvia was gone.

And here was Agnes. I looked at her looking at New Jersey while standing on top of a fake Ireland after drinking Irish car bombs in a fake Irish pub. She was a beautiful and imposing woman, a woman who demanded attention, who demanded to be seen in the here and now. I suddenly felt guilty for being there with her, in her yellow vintage dress, like I was betraying Sylvia, or Sylvia's memory, as if Sylvia were dead. Sylvia wasn't dead, of course, or she probably wasn't dead, and there was nothing to betray. I barely knew Sylvia. I wasn't dating her.

Agnes was saying something about Disney World. "I love it there," she said. Her eyes were big and green and so open. "I know it's not cool, but I love it. I went there when I was a kid and I was hooked. I was obsessed with Minnie Mouse. I still am, a little. There's something about her, the polka-dot dress and those shoes. I would totally wear that."

"I think she's supposed to be a flapper," I said.

"Well, no wonder," said Agnes, "so am I!" She trotted down the path.

We turned away from the river toward Spring Street. Agnes told me about her band in college. It was named after a big graffiti in town, "God Is Luv" with a *u*, L-u-v.

"What instrument did you play?" I asked.

"Oh, guitar, a little, and I sing. I don't really play anymore. Mostly I just liked the idea of being in a band. I like making up band names and band fashions. I guess I'm more of a conceptual musician," she said. She laughed out loud, a delightful laugh. It echoed across the empty cobblestone streets.

At a nearby Portuguese restaurant, we ordered vinho verde, which seemed the perfect thing to drink on a humid night after the Hunger Memorial: like water, but better. We ate tiny clams cooked with a spicy linguiça sausage. And a baby octopus salad with olives, caper berries, and celery. I split open the head with my knife and black ink squirted straight into my face. Some hit me in the cheek. I got a little on my glasses. The octopus was perfectly tender and warm, with a touch of lemon and a hint of the sea. Agnes ate eagerly and ordered more wine before we were through. We added some boquerones, little white anchovies, and some cured meats. I took my time and considered each bite.

Agnes told me about her theatrical aspirations. Part of her wanted to be avant-garde, she said, to make some real art, to do something meaningful, to be interesting. "But really," she said, "I want to be a movie star.

"There, I told you my dirty little secrets," she said. "I love Disney World and I'm dying to be famous. Your turn."

"Hmm," I said, "I don't know what my secrets are. I guess I don't have any."

"Jesus," Agnes said. "That's totally unfair. You're so blank. You're a blank man. I have no idea what you're thinking. You just sit there, silently judging me. Taking notes. For all I know, you are a serial killer."

"I love the show *Happy Days*," I blurted. "As a kid I really loved the Fonz. I had a lunch box. Does that make me more of a serial killer? Or less?"

"Henry Winkler?" she said. "Definitely more."

I told her my favorite bit of Fonzie trivia: His father abandoned the family when he was young, leaving his son only one thing: a lockbox. But it was locked and Fonzie didn't have a key. So he rode over it with his tricycle again and again until he finally cracked it.

"Guess what was inside?"

"I don't know. Leather underwear?"

"No. The key to the box. That was all that was in the lockbox."

"Jesus," Agnes said. "That was his dad's present? No wonder the Fonz was such a macho dick."

Agnes and I went for a nightcap at the Ear Inn, an ancient pub that felt like a fisherman's cave. We sat out by the street. The moonlight crossed the Hudson. Conversations rang around us like a mariachi band. I'd always liked those little guitars. I imagined Agnes playing one, wearing a little hat. I wanted to kiss her. She was full of some energy. It felt dangerous. I felt maybe she wanted to be kissed, or maybe she just had a way about her. She was an actress. She kept mentioning the magazine, and I had that feeling, a feeling of power and disempowerment combined, that I get when people will talk to me because they know where I work, like they want something from me, some media power I don't really have and don't really want. I thought of Magdalena again and tried not to.

"You have that face again, blank man," she said. "What are you thinking about now?"

The eternal question.

"Come on," she said. "Don't be shy."

"I'm thinking about these two guys that work at the farmers market with Sylvia," I said. "Luis and Warren."

"Oh, yeah," Agnes said, "the drug dealers."

I must have looked surprised.

"You haven't heard?" she said. "I think those guys supposedly deal Oxy out of the truck."

"Oxy?" I asked. "Like OxyContin?"

"Yeah, OxyContin or oxycodone or whatever you call it. It's all the rage. My dad had it when he got his knee replaced, and he was, like, out of his gourd when he had to stop taking it. He says he never felt anything like that."

"Are you sure?"

"I'm sure my dad is crazy. But I never bought any Oxy or any-thing. It's just something I heard. There's a whole network. They get the stuff from this quack in New Jersey. Some New Age guru."

"A guru?"

"That's what I heard."

"Sylvia knows about this?" I asked.

Agnes shrugged. "I'm sure she does. You know Sylvia."

# Chapter 22

# A GADFLY

By the end of the week, I'd gotten most of the checking done for "Mandeville/Green." I had talked to the director of the Green-markets and the president of the Council on the Environment of New York City, as well as a number of vendors. I had read articles and reports. I spoke with the USDA and with a professor at Rutgers. I'd also learned a lot about Sylvia. I found her last name and then had gone into People Search on LexisNexis (which wasn't strictly legal) and found many of her previous addresses. I found a lot of information about her friends from the Heads and Tails Supper Club, including Agnes; I found out more about Nick and the others at New Egypt; I found an ex-boyfriend, some kind of "environmental artist"; I found Sylvia's mother, who was no longer a hippie but a corporate lawyer at Baker Botts, a Houston law firm. They represented Big Oil. But I didn't find out anything about drugs at Union Square or a New Age guru or where Sylvia was or how to reach her.

I was also busy with other things, of course. On Friday afternoon I had to confirm a ridiculous quote from Donald Rumsfeld about how the war was essentially over in Afghanistan. "The Taliban are gone. The Al Qaeda are gone," he supposedly told Larry King. "There are people who are throwing hand grenades and shooting off rockets and trying to kill people, but there are people who are trying to kill people in New York or San Francisco. So it's not going to be a perfectly tidy place." It seemed like something Rumsfeld would say; he was always lying or deluded or both. But I hadn't been able to find the full quote anywhere. A few newspapers cited the interview generally. That didn't help. I needed the exact words, and it would be best if they came from the actual program, not some secondhand source, and I needed it by the end of the day. I couldn't find a recording of the show online. Back then, YouTube did not exist. Nor could I find a transcript on LexisNexis, so I had called a friend at CNN. He would dig up the transcript and send it over, he said. Give him an hour.

While I was waiting for my friend, I received an email from Jarvis. He answered my follow-up questions. Yes, New Egypt sells three varieties of eggplant, and, yes, they sell at Union Square all year, and, no, they don't employ migrant laborers (I was fishing with this question). And, sorry, he doesn't have a contact number for Sylvia.

"She had to leave the institute suddenly," he wrote, "to take care of some personal business." He wasn't sure when she'd be back, but he would forward contact info as soon as he heard from her. She had done a lot of good work for New Egypt, Jarvis wrote, and he hoped she'd return.

"But I'm not holding my breath," he wrote. "Sylvia is sort of a gadfly."

A gadfly?

I didn't know what he meant by that and what it had to do with holding one's breath. Maybe he was misusing the term *gadfly* or implying something about her. Maybe she was some kind of whistleblower who'd found out about the drug guru and was now persona non grata at the farm.

I read through "Mandeville/Green" again. I'd already checked off everything about New Egypt: farmers markets, CSAs, and some small farms were "booming." This was a reasonable claim. After walking around the market and talking to the young, idealistic growers of things, you could tell that there was a new back-to-the-land movement in America, and that it was popular. I knew from my research that some farms had been economically revived by farmers markets and that others, which may have been impossible without direct-to-consumer systems, had been founded under this new economic model. New Egypt was one of those. The passage was fine, but something nagged at me. This wasn't the whole story. The number of small farms in America had been rapidly and steadily decreasing for decades. Meanwhile, the number of gigantic farms, those that might be called "industrial," had skyrocketed and not just because of scale. Regulations and subsidies for the most part favored factory farms. Commodity-related grants, for example, were given only for crops like corn and soybeans, crops that are generally grown in huge quantities. These subsidies were also tied to output, encouraging an intensive, mass-production model and discouraging more environmentally friendly, low-yield uses of land. When farm subsidies or programs were mentioned, opponents liked to point out that the idea of the poor struggling farmer—Willie Nelson's Farm Aid victim—was a myth. The median household income for farmers was higher than that of average American households. True. But that income was largely concentrated in the largest, most profitable farms. Small farms tended to lose money, and those that did make money were not usually growers of fruits and vegetables or other "high-value" crops like New Egypt. These required too much labor cost; they could be finicky; they could really ruin the farmer without deep pockets or some other form of income. The owners of most small farms earned more off the farm than they did on it. They all had second jobs—like selling OxyContin. Sure, Jarvis had turned labor into "education" and rounded up donations from bankers and CEOs. But what did they want in return?

I turned to page three and the quote from Sylvia about "nefarious business." It was one of the few things I hadn't checked off. I reread the part where Mandeville mentioned some suspicions and infighting among the vendors—I had checked these carefully. There was definitely infighting. Some vendors suspected that others bought things wholesale, rather than growing everything—and then he threw in this somewhat randomly: *"One vendor said there was a lot of 'nefarious business' at the market. 'People sell everything here,' she said. 'It ain't all green.'"* Sylvia probably was not talking about OxyContin or a drug network or a crooked guru or the failure of a utopian dream. Nothing here was worth "skipping town" over. I knew I should just cross it off. I didn't. Would Sylvia say *ain't*? It didn't ring true.

I found myself staring at the ceiling again, thinking about Rumsfeld and his nonsense about "known unknowns" and "unknown unknowns," which somehow were both justifications for attacking Iraq. For Rumsfeld it didn't matter what you knew. Either knowledge or a lack of knowledge could serve as a pretext for war. There were so many unknown unknowns, after all. You better just lash out. Control the narrative. Kill. I had so many "unknown unknowns" of my own about Sylvia, and now I had a bunch of "intelligence," as Rumsfeld might call it, email addresses, suspicions. And a rumor: drug dealers at the Greenmarket. A drug guru. For all I knew, Sylvia was involved. What would I do if I found out this was true? Check off the quote.

Yes, "nefarious business" indeed. I thought of Hannah, the art assistant whose brother was a drug addict. I'd talked to her about him after the Billy Bragg show. I'd offered some comfort to her. Then she flipped me the bird.

A gadfly?

I called Mandeville again. He'd been avoiding me. He said he'd been "off the grid," living with homesteaders for his new piece. Then when we had a phone appointment, he had canceled it, saying he "had to tend to the girls." I didn't know what that meant, but he said it in a way that implied that I would know what he meant. This was the kind of thing Mandeville did. He was an interpolator. This phrase *tend to the girls* sounded a bit misogynist or dismissive. His girls—he was married to a young, indie-famous actress and had an infant daughter—needed tending like livestock, I thought. This must have been language he'd picked up from the homesteaders, who probably homeschooled their children and insisted on archaic gender roles. But then maybe I wasn't being very charitable. Perhaps Mandeville was finally spending time with his wife and daughter when he was usually too busy with work or hunting or eating or drinking, and maybe the homesteaders were completely open-minded or even radically feminist. Some nineteenth-century communes were. Mandeville probably knew his piece wasn't going to press soon. It wasn't urgent. He couldn't have suspected that I was anxious about Sylvia's disappearance or the possibility of drugs.

I left another voicemail.

I waited for a while without doing anything, really. I stared at the ceiling again. I realized I was hungry, but I didn't want anything to eat—at least, not anything that I could get my hands on at that moment; not an industrial sandwich from the cafeteria. I wanted a tomato with salt. A Brandywine or a Mortgage Lifter. I thought about what it might be like to be a drug addict itching for a fix.

I called Sylvia's mom at the Houston law firm and left a message: I was calling about a fact-checking matter. It was urgent.

A half hour later my phone rang.

It wasn't Mandeville or Sylvia or her mom.

It was my CNN friend. He sent over the transcript. I scanned it carefully.

Check. Check. Check.

It was true: Rumsfeld was an asshole.

# Chapter 23

# MAO ZEDONG

I had gone looking for Magdalena once. It was the beginning of the end for us, or maybe it was the middle of the end for us. She hadn't returned my calls for a few days. This in itself wasn't that strange. Even though Magda and I basically lived together at that point and shared most of our meals, there were many occasions when she would disappear, sometimes for a few days. Then she'd resurface and things would go on as before. We rarely talked about these silences. Magda didn't offer much of an explanation. She was always a strange combination of demandingly self-possessed and emotionally fragile. She depended on me in ways that, I think, made both of us uncomfortable. Maybe she couldn't bear that dependence at times and had to get away from me. Or maybe she simply couldn't bear me. Or maybe it had nothing to do with me; she seemed so inaccessible during these spells that I just pretended they didn't happen. In retrospect I should have demanded more of her, or asked her more questions, or cared more for her, or something.

It was an April evening, 1999, when I went looking for her. I had been out of town for a few days—here in New York, actually. I was hoping to move here. This was one of our problems, but not the main one. When I returned, I immediately knew something was wrong.

She had been silent for days. I kept driving by her house. She wasn't there and neither was her car, a blue Ford Taurus. Suddenly I had to find her. I drove around to every place that she might be, to Pops and to August and to the Whole Foods. There were blue Tauruses but not hers. I circled all the likely neighborhoods and dropped by her friend Angie's house and the library. I stopped at Rusty's and had two quick drinks. I'd already had a whiskey at home and was feeling it as I got back in my car. I was on the edge of drunk, I thought, and then I realized that once you think you are on the edge, you are probably over the edge, but I was already driving to her advisor Frank's house. My ex-advisor. Her blue Taurus was parked in front. I waited across the street. There was only one room lit in the house, and I couldn't see anything. I just sat there. For about forty-two minutes I sat there. Nothing happened.

I went home.

I filled a thermos with whiskey and water and ice and went for a walk around campus, getting drunker and more miserable by the minute. In part I felt hurt and angry and betrayed by Magda, but mostly I was racked with an acute sense of shame for sneaking around, suspicious. Just because she was parked at Frank's house didn't mean anything. We'd both been there many times. Magda often did research for him. She had even watched his kids once or twice. She didn't have to call me back. Not calling someone back doesn't justify crazy ideas about betrayal or stalker behavior. What kind of person was I to drunkenly stake out my own girlfriend?

Of course, my suspicions were proven right in the end. She did leave me for Frank the Fraud. But I still felt ashamed of my behavior even after I was vindicated. *Vindicated* has the same root as *vindictive*, a terrible thing to be.

\* \* \*

And here I was again, stalking a woman—or stalking her workplace, at least. I wasn't vindictive, not exactly, nor did I think that Warren and Luis, the alleged drug dealers, would lead me to Sylvia. But I was suspicious, for sure. I had to know what was what. My plan at first, insofar as I had a plan, was to chat with McDonough to see if he knew anything about a drug-dealing "network" or this "guru" or anything more about Sylvia "skipping town." But McDonough wasn't there—he'd gone to check out a new Greenmarket in Harlem—so I browsed Sanders's stand and couldn't quite imagine him getting a blow job. Thank god. I talked to Marshall at Stokes. I talked to Nick. No news. I did a few laps around the park. I didn't see any drug dealers, not that I knew what they might look like unless they looked like Warren, the guy with the billy goat beard. I didn't see him either. Not at first. Instead I saw a guy wearing one of those extra-long shirts that said CHOOSE LIFE in giant letters. I saw the most incredible tiny strawberries. I saw a kid do a kickflip and actually land it.

Eventually I walked back around to Stokes Farms, talked to Marshall again, and to a flower girl named Beth. She knew Sylvia a little but hadn't seen her in a few weeks. "What a cool lady," she said, smiling sweetly.

"Cool lady," I repeated like an idiot. "She mentioned something to me," I said, "about a black market at the farmers market?"

"What, like, stolen apples?"

I shrugged.

She shrugged.

Then she started giggling. She tried to suppress her laugh but couldn't. She was looking at me funny. I checked my fly. Up.

I read the flower names: zinnias, rudbeckia, scabiosa.

"None of them were stolen," she said. And she began to laugh again.

Finally, I left the market. I ate lunch at a popular place across Park Avenue called Zen Palate. I wondered how your palate could be Zen. Perhaps you might taste everything and nothing at once. It turned out that Zen Palate just tasted like nothing. At least to me. Maybe I had the wrong ideas about Zen.

I crossed the park, heading for the subway—I was going to head home—when I spotted Warren unpacking boxes. He really *did* look suspicious. I found a bench with a good view of the New Egypt stand. I saw Luis too. He started helping Warren. They were sitting close together. For a while I just watched.

I don't know how long I had been sitting on the park bench when that stakeout of Magda came back to me, bringing some bile along with it. Was I repeating myself? If I wanted to stalk Sylvia, I'd have to find her, and I wasn't going to find her by watching two possible drug dealers at the one place where no one had seen Sylvia. I didn't even know if the drug dealers had anything to do with Sylvia's cryptic fears about the farmers market and her "skipping town," leaving her farm behind. I didn't really know what I'd do if I saw something, just like I didn't know what I'd do if I saw Magdalena at Frank's house, which I didn't really see, only the car, and yet on that park bench I felt a little of that awful feeling that night, a feeling that something had taken hold of me and I had to follow.

A guy with long hair and cargo shorts sat down on the bench right next to mine. "I'm at the farmers market," he said into his phone. "The farmers market," he shouted. "Don't worry, it's done," he said forcefully. "It's done. Trust me."

What's done? I thought. The way he had said, "Don't worry, it's done," reminded me of a gangster in a movie telling his boss that he's offed someone. Don't worry, he tells his boss, your worries are over, or at least those particular worries associated with that person you wanted out of the way, you wanted rubbed out, dead. Criminals keep it vague: they don't say the obvious, they don't say, "Yes, sir, I killed the guy you paid me to kill and now you don't have to worry about him ratting you out or betraying you"; they just say, "Don't worry, it's done."

I looked up at New Egypt again. Warren was there talking intently to a fat man. I watched as Warren and the fat guy wandered away from the stand. After a brief discussion, it looked like the man handed Warren something. Was it an envelope? I couldn't be sure. Then he left. Warren walked over to Luis and said something to him. Nick and Tina were helping customers. Luis took a few empty crates and loaded them into the truck, hopping inside. When he came out he was carrying a backpack, which he handed to Warren. Warren put something in the backpack and then put it back in the truck.

I ate an apricot Nick had sold me, half price.

I saw Warren leaving. He was wearing the backpack. He waved at the others. I decided to follow him.

I tailed him into the subway. As I passed through the turnstile, I saw him approaching the L train. I had to hurry to keep up. Luckily there were a lot of other people hurrying too. I stayed behind a doughy guy in a white polo. Warren was quick. He was already boarding the train when I leaped down the last few stairs. The doors closed. I missed it. Then they opened again. I squeezed in. It was like a muffin tin of flesh in there. I caught sight of the billy goat beard. We rode to Eighth Avenue, the last stop. I got out ahead of Warren and swam slowly among the sea of people. I knew he'd be going the same way at least to the top of the stairs. I pretended to look closely at the Tom Otterness bronze sculptures hanging on to parts of the staircase. They looked like little elves conspiring on some secret project—for good or evil, I didn't know. I caught sight of the mud-colored shirt. I followed. We boarded the uptown C train. It was less crowded now so I decided to get on a different car than Warren, but I parked myself near the door, ready to deboard when he did. It turned out, though, to be a difficult operation. I had to get out at every stop to let people by, and then it was rude to stop right at the door as people were piling on behind me. I generally like to observe subway etiquette. A Chinese man stood very close to me after Twenty-Third Street. He wore a peculiar kind of hip engineer's hat, almost a Mao hat, but not quite. I liked it. I wondered if in China this hat had some cultural meaning, a meaning I could never read. Was he even from China or was that my prejudiced assumption? He was very close to me. Could I push my elbows out, I wondered, to create a larger bubble of space around me? Thirty-Fourth Street. I saw Warren's backpack. Black JanSport. I followed it down into Penn Station. We stayed on the subterranean level, moving through the belly of the station. We passed denuded fast-food stands, Nathan's hot dogs, Dunkin' Donuts, Knot Just Pretzels. At the end of the hall a faux old-time band was playing. I could just barely hear the clarinet and the washboards. I could see the band members in jaunty hats. The sound of the banjo clanged together with the din of the station, and amid the strange orange lighting I had the sense of being inside an oven, specifically the rotisserie oven that we had in the office because someone had written a story about it, and they sent it to the checking department. (Set it and forget it.) A young woman, moonfaced in a red dress, stood up to sing. Her wavering voice cut across the oven waves.

"Hope is a thing with feathers," she sang, "that perches in the soul."

I followed Warren past the Long Island Rail Road ticket window into a bar I'd never noticed. It was called Tracks. One of the bartenders, a chipper blonde with a squirrel tattoo on her shoulder, waved at him. Warren raised his wild beard in recognition and took a seat halfway down the narrow room looking back toward me, fifteen feet behind, as he did so. I ducked my head instinctively toward the bar, stumbling into a large, soft shoulder. A head turned toward me. A large soft person was connected to it. "Sorry," I said. I looked back toward Warren. He was talking to the blonde, paying me no mind. She set some kind of drink in front of him—not beer, not whiskey, I wasn't sure what—and made her way down the bar. I ordered a Brooklyn Lager and took it to the long counter on the opposite wall. From there I could see Warren but stayed out of his direct line of sight. I could also see the Mets game. When I moved to New York, I became a Mets fan. The Yankees were very good at the time, as they often were. But I couldn't just start rooting for the Yankees, the rich, the powerful, the privileged. The Mets were more appealing with their cartoon blue and their nonromanticized stadium; they were underdogs, the working class. They were playing the Braves, and when I entered Tracks, were already down 1–0. The bases were loaded for Julio Franco, Atlanta's ageless slugger. Things didn't look good, but Al Leiter threw a slow curve, and Franco grounded to short. Double play. Nobody scored.

Warren wasn't talking to anyone. He wasn't watching baseball. He was just drinking. He had another round. And another. The bar around him bristled with the come and go of commuters and tourists. A gaggle of twentysomething girls, heavily made up, gathered in the space between us. They were talking about how unbelievable something was. "Unbelievable," said one. "Unbelievable," said another. The Mets tied the game on a sharp single to center field. I drank another beer and looked at the raw bar menu. Oysters in the bowels of Penn Station sounded like a bad idea, but there were a bunch of positive newspaper clips about them. I got a half dozen Malpeques, slathered them in mignonette, and slurped one down. It was briny and firm, perfectly like the sea. I imagined myself in Iceland with Sylvia, surrounded by volcanic cliffs. It was the bottom of the fifth when José Reyes hit a swinging bunt to the pitcher and beat the throw to first. He stole second. Kazuo Matsui moved him over to third, and when Cliff Floyd hit a grounder, he broke for home. There was no way he could make it, but Reyes, the gray fox with the narrow eyes and the wicked legs, was going all out. I felt myself stand up. Reyes slid headfirst as the catcher swung his mitt across the dirt. Reyes was already beyond him. Safe: 2–1 Mets. I looked up at the bartender with the squirrel tattoo. She threw back her dyed hair and opened her mouth, laughing. I felt a weird surge of joy, there in the train station bar.

When I turned, I saw Warren looking right at me. I had almost forgotten about him. He held me in his gaze, his wild beard pointed toward me, as if in anger. I grabbed nervously for my beer and looked back up at the TV. Warren got up and walked right toward me. He kept me in his gaze. He walked slowly and purposefully. He came close, a few feet away, still looking at me sternly, then passed and headed out of the bar. He didn't say anything. Neither did I.

I went after him, but it took me a moment to gather myself. By the time I reached the exit, he was gone, wild beard, backpack, and all.

Disappeared.

# Chapter 24

# CLEARVIEW

A few days later, I found myself tailing someone else. At the time I was working on a "Hazlin/Casual" that had come in that morning and needed to close by the end of day. Even though it seemed simple, it required some care so I had to get right to work. "You know Hazlin," Charles said when he handed it off. I knew Hazlin.

Of course, everyone knows Hazlin. When people hear I work for the magazine, they always ask me about Hazlin. He's been writing for the magazine since the 1960s and is definitely among our most popular writers. "I like Hazlin," I tell them, trying to sound nonchalant, trying to brag without bragging. "He's a lot like you'd expect." Although Hazlin was in his sixties and was a giant man, probably three hundred pounds, he had a childlike enthusiasm. I couldn't fault him for that.

But what Charles meant when he said, "You know Hazlin," was this: Hazlin was probably the least accurate writer I had ever dealt with. This was another thing I told people, bragging without wanting to brag: Even though his stories barely had any facts in them—they were often just riffs—whatever facts they had were usually wrong. One had to be very careful to check even the most obvious things. I'd once let a mistake through when he mixed up the characters of *The Great Gatsby* in a little piece on Fitzgerald. It was going to press quickly, and in my haste I had just assumed his descriptions of Jordan and Daisy were correct, since they seemed fundamental to what he was writing and they squared with my memory of the novel. But he'd actually transposed the characters, Daisy for Jordan and vice versa, and then added a few totally fabricated attributes to each. The mistake was my fault, of course. It's the fact-checker and not the famous writer who is responsible for these things. That's the way checking works.

Hazlin stopped by my desk just after Charles dropped the piece. I thought he was going to give me some helpful information about his piece, but he didn't. "Big Papi," he said, "is absolutely indomitable. Is he not?" Hazlin was referring to David Ortiz, the Dominican slugger for the Red Sox. "I love to watch him," he went on, blinking away incessantly. "He has this insouciance," Hazlin said, "the way he lumbers up to the plate, yet there is this twinkle in his eye. The BoSox will take the pennant," he added. "Big Papi will lead them there. You can bet on it."

"Well," I said. I paused for a minute, thinking about the idea of the pennant, the flag itself. "I'm not sure about the bullpen," I said.

But Hazlin, the old, giant man, was already skipping down the hall. "The bullpen will hold, my friend," he shouted over his shoulder.

This was a typical exchange. Hazlin was an essayist. He liked to make proclamations, and before I might respond, he was gone. I actually enjoyed these presumptuous little lectures even when he used words like *insouciance*, which sounded odd when spoken aloud and even odder when spoken casually about a power hitter, or when he self-consciously deployed baseball nicknames like "Big Papi," sounding like a kid trying out slang for the first time. He carried all this off with a goofy glee, like it was just a game. And, I suppose, it was.

Without much information from Hazlin, I met with Oliver, the editor who reworked all the Casuals so they conformed to a standardized formula. "You'll never guess what Hazlin said when he turned in this piece," Oliver told me. "He said, 'It's all written. Now all it needs is the facts.'" Oliver thought this was hilarious. "All it needs is the facts," he said again, waiting for me to laugh too. I kept him waiting.

The missing facts, in this case, had to do with a transformation of New York City's street signs. There was a new font and design and new larger signs on the bigger avenues. This was a sad turn of events for nostalgic Hazlin. It signaled the death of the old city, the rise of Big Box Manhattan, a town beholden to the bland, alien motorist and not the quirky local pedestrian. It was a nice piece.

I called the DOT and after a bit of runaround I confirmed that there was a change taking place and that the change was part of a federal mandate that would take more than a decade and some $20 million to implement. The city had to comply. Its hands were tied. None of this was in the article, so I took careful notes and repeated them back to the officials. The piece also described a few specific street signs. I couldn't trust Hazlin with the details, and the DOT said they'd have to get back to me. But I knew not to trust the government to get back to me within two hours, no matter how many different people I called. I gave them all my cell phone number and headed out to the streets to check for myself.

I was nearing one of the intersections Hazlin described when I saw Sylvia. Or I thought I did. She was already on the other side of the subway stairwell at Sixty-Eighth Street, and there were dozens of people, mostly young and pierced, teeming out of the train, crowding between us. I quickened my pace. I got close to her just as she turned east down Sixty-Eighth Street, the same direction I was headed. I scooted around some slow walkers and got within a few feet of her. I could see her long fingers. They had the same small spindly quality as Sylvia's although they now had a coat of garnet polish. Weren't Sylvia's nails unpolished? It couldn't be Sylvia.

I thought about calling out to the woman. I could shout out "Sylvia" and then apologize; "I thought you were someone else," I'd say. Perhaps she would say, "Oh, no, don't worry," and we would begin a conversation about people for whom we were mistaken. I could tell her that people say I look like Tony Shalhoub, the actor. This wasn't exactly flattering, but I liked Tony Shalhoub. Maybe this girl, this Sylvia look-alike, wouldn't know who Tony Shalhoub was. If it actually was Sylvia, she might not know either. We could discuss. I didn't call out; I just followed, even though I knew I should do some better version of surveillance than I did when I tried to follow Warren.

I got close to her as we crossed Second Avenue, close enough to hear her breathe. She was dressed well, not like a person who grew up on a commune and works on a farm and is interested in cults, a person who wants to worship the Deity, who is trying to do good without intervening too much. She didn't look like the utopian type, if that is a type, if that type has a certain handbag and a certain way of being-in-the-world.

I decided to pass her and to face her head-on. I was already two blocks past where I should have turned to check Hazlin's signs. I rushed ahead and, at the corner of First Avenue, paused as if I had forgotten something and spun around. But the woman wasn't behind me anymore. I had passed her only a few seconds before. She must have slipped into a building or darted across the street. I looked everywhere. She was gone, gone for a Burton and gone for a shit with a rug around her. Disappeared.

When I got back to my desk the phone was ringing. I rushed to grab it. It wasn't Sylvia. It was Tony Curtis. His piece had already gone to press and there was no reason for him to call me.

"I'm just checking in," he said. "I have to go to the dentist today so you won't be able to reach me."

I reassured him that I had everything I needed, but apparently I also needed to hear about his dental history. His dentist was beautiful. So were his implants.

In Oliver's office, we went through my Hazlin notes. Hazlin, not surprisingly, had gotten most of the details about the signs wrong. He'd said the signs had gone from lowercase to all caps. The reverse was actually true. He'd said the signs were looming above streets, yards before intersections; they weren't. Oliver and I made the changes. We added that the old font Highway Gothic was being replaced by one with the *Brave New World*–ish name of "Clearview." We reversed the things that needed to be reversed. Surprisingly, though, Hazlin's main ideas stood. Perhaps this was a sign that they were not very deep ideas. Or that they were. I couldn't decide. New York, Hazlin thought, should be a city for people who already know where they are. When you're on Park Avenue, you know it. You don't need some big sign to tell you.

I knew the city well. I knew where I was most of the time. But there was still so much hidden, I thought, as I read the final galley proofs. There were no signs pointing me in the direction of Sylvia. I had no good theories or ideas about her—at least, none that arose from the evidence present. All I was doing was tailing people, and I was clearly really bad at it. I needed a new tactic. I signed off on Hazlin's piece, now completely rewritten sentence by sentence, and headed back to the Greenmarket. I was going to check some facts.

# Chapter 25

# YO, CHIEF

Union Square hadn't always been a park. In the early eighteenth century, the plot of land at the corner of Bloomingdale and Bowery Roads was a potter's field. But in the 1790s, the city government decided it needed a new hanging and burial ground. It bought a plot of land to the southwest called Washington Square (against the objections of local landowner Alexander Hamilton). This freed up Union Square, already overloaded with anonymous cadavers, to become a public green. Around the same time, Madison Square too made the transition from potter's field to public park. By the 1820s, Washington Square followed suit. The anonymous dead were shipped uptown to the plot near Times Square, now Bryant Park, the park I could see out my office windows. Like so many other public parks in the city, it turns out, it was built on a foundation of corpses.

I couldn't help thinking about this as I was circling the park that evening. I had come there to ask Nick more directly about Oxy and "the guru" and to see if he might know more than he was letting on. Not that I had much hope. I wasn't really sure what to say to him. "Nick, are you hiding something? It says here you are selling drugs." It didn't say that anywhere. It probably wasn't true. Nick, in any case, was busy when I arrived. There were a lot of customers around, and he was moving maniacally from task to task, so I just loitered. I watched customers. Nobody stole anything. Nobody landed any kickflips.

Warren was over by the truck. I didn't want to talk to *him*. I didn't even want him to see me. I felt like he was staring at me, though, even when he was out of sight, like he had at Tracks. I was paranoid. So I walked away from the stand. I did a circle down past the Gandhi statue, over past Stokes. I passed some folks with political signs: NO BLOOD FOR OIL. I tried not to think about all the dead people beneath me.

Eventually, I circled back to New Egypt. I didn't see Warren or Nick, but I did see Luis. He was sitting off to the side of the stand, sifting through greens, throwing scraps into a bin. He was wearing his customary purple bandana and purple high-tops. The black JanSport backpack was on the ground beside him. I approached and then just hovered there, unsure. He didn't say anything. I didn't say anything either, not till it seemed like he'd picked through several boxes of greens and I thought, wow, that's a lot of wasted greens.

"Hey," I finally squeaked.

He still didn't say anything. I wasn't sure how to ask him about selling drugs. I'd never really asked a stranger for drugs. I remembered a time in high school when I spent a weekend with my friend's brother in the city. He called a marijuana delivery service. They would answer the phone, "Yo, chief." And you had to reply "Yo, chief"—that was the code—so they'd know you were cool. Then they'd send a blue sedan, always a blue sedan.

"Yo, chief," I said to Luis.

He looked at me like I was an idiot.

"Are you selling anything?" I said.

"Uh, yeah," he said, "look around."

"Look around," I said.

"Something wrong with you, man?"

This wasn't going anywhere.

"Don't I know you from somewhere?" he said.

"I'm a friend of Sylvia's," I said.

"You from Seattle?" he asked. "DAN?"

"Yep," I said, "Dan," just to be agreeable.

He jumped up and grabbed his Black JanSport. He pulled out a piece of paper and handed it to me. It was a flier with a grainy photo of a barge and some text underneath. It read:

BLACKWATER

ON

THE DISPOSSESSED

Direct Action Planning + Party

August 7

7 p.m.

1st St & the Gowanus Canal.

(Don't cut through the lot at the end of 1st Street.

That would be trespassing! . . . But if you do,

watch out for the rusty tire irons)

DJ Zapata

and maybe a keg

"I'll be there," I said.

# Chapter 26

# BLACKWATER

To get to the *Dispossessed*, an old Navy rescue boat moored on the Gowanus Canal, you had to squeeze through a gap in a chain-link fence and cross an empty lot littered with tall weeds and rusty debris. The boat, which a group of anarchists had salvaged and turned into a "community space," was tied up there. There was no dock, so I climbed up onto the wooden retaining wall and then stretched my leg and lumbered aboard. It wasn't easy, and for a moment I thought I might slip into the impossibly polluted Gowanus Canal, which smelled terrible and looked dark and greasy. Luckily a guy in a handlebar mustache came over and helped me aboard. What was with all these young men with elaborate mustaches? I wondered. Not that handlebar mustaches were so bad. They were certainly no worse than my ragged two-day stubble and my lack of any discernible style, and besides, this guy had just helped me out, even if he might be an ironically stylish anarchist, which seemed, in some way, a contradiction.

"You're here for the meeting?" he said, and gestured to a doorway.

I entered a long, low wooden room cut with arrows of dusty light from the setting sun and filled with people, most of them sitting on the ground. I found a spot in the back. A vigorous discussion was going on among a few of the activists near the center of the room.

It was hard to follow. They used acronyms and code names and kept mentioning the marathon table and the oil spill. I spotted Luis sitting in the opposite corner, surrounded by a group of young women. I glanced over at him, but he didn't look my way. Two others did: a tall thin redheaded man and a shorter guy with a shaved head were staring at me, nasty looks. Was I intruding? Did I look like a narc? I looked over at Luis again, hoping to catch his eye. He ignored me. The skinhead was still looking at me, though, not smiling.

The rest of the crowd consisted mostly of young people, shaggy but collegiate-looking young people. A few mustaches. A few long beards. No Sylvia. In the center of the circle was an older woman who seemed to be in charge. She had frizzy gray hair and she spoke very quietly so that you had to strain to hear her. This had the paradoxical effect of commanding respect and deference. Maybe she just had a presence, like Mandeville. In any case, she was good at cutting people off. She listened intently and then seemed to know the exact moment to interrupt and move things along. It was fairly impressive, especially given that some people had a lot to say, even if it wasn't worth saying.

After a while I caught on to the gist of the meeting. The activists—I knew from my research that the *Dispossessed* was the headquarters of a group of radical environmentalists, "Green Anarchists"—were planning a street-theater protest at the RNC, which would arrive in New York in three weeks. The main idea was to bring one hundred gallons or more of polluted Gowanus water packaged in plastic bottles and branded BLACKWATER—SUPERFUND SPRINGS—GOWANUS to the area around the Hilton Hotel where many delegations, including the Texas group, would be staying. The details of the protest were under debate. Some wanted to scale the side of the hotel at night and to unfurl a giant banner advertising the amazing BLACKWATER CURE ALL and celebrating the environmental, economic, and military evils of the administration. Some also wanted to pour gallons of dirty water into the lobby. But others were opposed to any pouring of water on anyone, as this might be an act of violence and a health hazard. There was some back-and-forth about this when Marlo, a guy with a mess of curly blond hair, shouted, "We're living in this shit. Look around you. And you are worried if a bunch of fucking capitalists will get a little dirt on their cowboy boots? Fuck that."

The moderator gave him a withering look, and he sat back down.

A guy who looked like a young James Spader then proposed that a group be formed to research the feasibility of the wall-climbing action. There was a lengthy back-and-forth about what the proposal actually meant: Was it a formal proposal or just a suggestion? Was the group independent or part of the larger coalition? A woman named Julie who wore round John Lennon glasses seemed set against the formation of any group and against any scaling of any walls. She asked exactly how the group would conduct its research and what they would do with this research, and would it be a form of power? Several others, including James Spader, spent time trying to convince her that the group would have limited duties, and in any case the group would be open if she wanted to join. Julie threatened to block the proposal, and the meeting went on and on for a long time, trying to determine whether to form a fact-finding group or not.

I felt myself getting sleepy. I had been excited at first to be somewhat randomly invited into a group of radical leftists on a boat—another cult?—where I might find Sylvia. But Sylvia wasn't there, and the bureaucratic nitpicking of it all had worn me down. Was this what anarchy was like? Lots of meetings to discuss tiny, meaningless things? Wasn't that what fact-checking was like too? It didn't help that I had poured myself a giant beer at the keg in back and that I had drunk most of it. I was now sipping something warm and flat as the sun had mostly receded and the room twinkled with string lights.

Across the room I saw Luis get up and head to the door. I took that as a cue to follow him.

I found him alone up near the bow, smoking something that looked like a fountain pen.

"What's the news from Seattle?" Luis asked me, handing me his pen. I'd given up smoking, but I wanted to be agreeable. I pressed the button and sucked. It tasted something like a pine tree, with a hint of marijuana. I suppressed a cough.

"I'm not from Seattle," I said.

"Then where you from, man?"

"New Jersey, actually."

"Me too," he said. "Somerset County." He laughed. "I bet you thought I was from Mexico. Everyone thinks that. If you look like me, man, and you work in the farmers market, that's what they assume. Or maybe Nicaragua. Or, like, Guatemala or where was it? Some migrant-worker place. Not like New Jersey. But it's so, like, Paraguay in Somerset County, man. It's Paraguay, New Jersey. Paraguay, not Uruguay, man," he said. "People always get that mixed up too." He was very chatty. Maybe stoned. "So what are you doing here?" he said. "You're not from the Seattle DAN?" I now knew he meant Direct Action Network.

"I thought Sylvia might be here."

"Sylvia," he repeated. "Righteous." He looked off across the putrid water. "Sylvia," he said again, as if he had just remembered her. "She came down here. Checking us out. She dug it but, like, wasn't into the meetings. It can be hard, like, at first, to get into the whole direct action thing," he said, "especially for women."

I wasn't sure what he meant by that, but I let it lie.

"But for me," he kept going, "there's no other way. In Paraguay, my parents lived under a dictator, but now it's, like, autopilot America, man. It's just tee times and annuities, you know? That sucks. After the shit that went down, that's still going down in Itaipu, but whatever." He paused and sucked on his device. "What do you think, man, of the action? Want to get involved?"

"I don't know. Won't you all get arrested?"

"Yeah. Probably. That's the idea."

"But why? Will it change anything?"

"Maybe not," Luis said, "but it's not always about changing people's minds. It's not just about other people; it's, like, an experience, you know, a ritual. How else are you supposed to live?"

I didn't have an answer for that.

I wanted to ask him about Warren and Oxy: Is that guy Warren a drug dealer? That might sound abrupt. Perhaps Warren was involved with the anarchists.

"Shit!" Luis shouted suddenly. "You are that magazine guy, aren't you? Don't tell anyone. If they find out you're a journalist—"

"I'm not—" I said.

"—they'll fuck you up," he said, and gave me a look. Serious. But then handed me the pen again as if it were a peace offering. I took a drag to make peace and looked where he was looking, over the water toward the lights on the edge of New York Harbor. I tried to look at the farthest light, and then to look farther.

"Kind of cool being on a boat," Luis said. "It's, like, freedom. No one to answer to." Luis stepped up onto the prow of the boat with one foot on each side and spread his arms like Leonardo DiCaprio in *Titanic*. I thought of the *Titanic* memorial and the American Venus and all the people who had drowned in the North Atlantic. Luis shouted, "I'm the king of the world." I suddenly felt really woozy. I had to step away from the water. I headed back toward the cabin, grabbing onto the wall as I went. People were coming up the stairs at this point, streaming by me. The meeting must have ended. I leaned against the wall and breathed, looking up at the sky. There was Orion, the Hunter. I wondered how long ago the stars I was seeing had existed, giving off this light, millions of years.

I stumbled back to the main room and had to take a moment for my brain to make sense of what I was seeing: In the middle of the room, where we had all been sitting, a crowd of activists wearing heavily padded white jumpsuits with white gas masks was jumping up and down. Apparently, this was the uniform for the protest, and they were trying it out. They looked insane, not just because of the weird alien getup, but also because they were trying to dance, and in all the taped-on padding they couldn't control their limbs. Some of them started falling over on purpose and rolling around. Others started flailing about wildly. It was quite funny to watch, these awkward marshmallow men, knocking each other over, laughing. "96 Tears" by Question Mark and the Mysterians was blasting, and they were jumping up and down to the beat, the organ driving them on. A bunch of other activists—it now felt like a lot more people were there—joined in, slamming into the padded jumpsuits. The floor of the boat was flexing and thumping; it felt like something was going to break. Everyone was dancing. I was mesmerized by these weird white suits and gas masks, jumping, bumping, falling, rolling, and the chaos around them, everyone leaping madly. Time passed strangely. They bounced. I drank. Surely I should stay here, I thought. Luis was right. How were you supposed to live? You were supposed to wear a

153

jumpsuit and a gas mask and jump up and down in unison. You were supposed to perform a ritual of resistance, even if the ritual was silly and pointless, and cry, cry, cry, ninety-six tears, but then I thought of that boring meeting, and Sylvia—where was she?—Let's do it, she'd said. Why hadn't I asked Luis about the drugs? Were the anarchists selling drugs? I'd never know. I was just hanging around on the fringes of things. Maybe they were cooking drugs. Is that the verb you use? Some drugs you have to "cook." Others, I suppose you refine or synthesize or something. Question Mark and the Mysterians were a Mexican American band, the children of migrant farmworkers in Saginaw, Michigan; the singer claimed his soul had come from Mars and that he'd walked with the dinosaurs. He might like this dance, and where was Sylvia? The music changed, and a wave hit me—the strong, putrid smell of the Gowanus. An overpowering gas smell. I tried to stand up for a moment but couldn't. I staggered. What had I smoked? Had it been cooked? I needed to breathe. I needed to pee. I stumbled up on deck.

"Yo," I heard. It startled me, but I was peeing off the side of the boat so I didn't turn around.

"Hey, man."

"I'm trying to take a piss here," I said.

I finished peeing and turned. It was the two menacing guys. The skinhead was close to me. I looked at his sweaty face. I smelled the Gowanus.

"That's pretty rude, man," the redhead said. "Do you think this is your toilet?"

"Sorry," I muttered.

"Who are you?" the skinhead said, stepping close to me, threatening.

"Are you a cop?"

"Or a reporter?"

"What's wrong with you man? Why are you so nervous?"

I looked down. I had peed on my pant leg.

"I—I," I stammered. The skinhead stepped closer, too close. I jumped.

That's the last thing I remember clearly from that night, the skinhead looking nastily at me as I teetered on the edge of the boat, and then I leaped off the boat. I suppose I made it to shore. I don't know if they gave chase. All I know for certain is this: I had a pretty bad gash on my shin the next morning; my pants were torn; my head was killing me.

And I still had no idea where Sylvia was or why she had disappeared.

# Chapter 27

# TWO TREES

Things didn't get any clearer that week. Nor did my shin feel better. Nor my head. Nor my soul. It didn't help that I had to spend a chunk of Monday reading a dense UN report about Afghanistan, trying to confirm, among other things, a reporter's claim that "heroin production has grown exponentially" since the invasion. The reporter had apparently heard it directly from his anonymous CIA source. I suspected the source was right but that he was using "exponentially" figuratively. That wasn't necessarily how it read in our piece so I was trying to determine if, say, there were ten acres of poppies in 2000, there were now at least a hundred acres. I found plenty of sources that mentioned growth, but none were precise. The UN report didn't seem to have any specifics either, but maybe it was me. I couldn't focus.

The phone rang. Restricted number. I had a moment of anticipation, as I had had every time the phone rang for the last three weeks. Sylvia? I picked up.

It wasn't Sylvia. It was her mother. I told her that we were running a story about the farmers market and that her daughter was a source. I had a few questions.

"It says here," I said, "that Sylvia grew up in Oregon on a commune called Two Trees. Is that right?"

"She probably made it sound just awful," Sylvia's mother said. "She's always been a complainer."

"Not at all," I said. "She spoke fondly—"

"What?" she interrupted. "Now she loves the community? Whatever I do, it's always wrong. Now she loves the community and hates Houston, hates my success."

"It says here you put yourself through law school," I said, trying to reboot the conversation.

"Are you seeing her?" Sylvia's mom asked. "You sound like her type."

"Excuse me?" I said.

"Is she happy?" Sylvia's mother said.

I paused.

I wanted to ask more questions about the commune, about the farming there and the division of labor and about whether she thought at all about what communal life had done for her, whether she still had ideals, utopian ideals, feminist ideals, perhaps, and how she lived with them now, in life, and in relationships.

"You don't know where I can reach her," I said, "do you?"

"No," Sylvia's mother said. And she began to cry.


I gave up on the poppy production after that. I wrote in the margins: "Unsure about 'exponential.' Suggested edit: 'Heroin production has soared.'"

# Chapter 28

# SUPERCONDUCTORS

The next night my search for Sylvia ended. More or less. I went to see Niko's band at Tonic. It was art-rock with a Balkan sound—marimbas and a theremin. I didn't know anyone at the show. This might normally have caused me discomfort, but I wanted to be alone in a crowd that night. The music was eerie, and it matched my mood. I stood, mostly against the brick wall, sipping my drink. I tried to ignore the throbbing in my shin and to let my mind drift. I pictured Sylvia's scar but then suddenly couldn't really picture the rest of her face. Only the scar. Why would a person just disappear, a beautiful person with communitarian tendencies, in the middle of tomato season? All her experiments were just now ripening. The clarinet and the theremin droned on like a pair of strange insects. I wondered who at the show might be on drugs and what kind. I knew nothing about this. If they were on Oxy, I wouldn't have the slightest idea. If they were anarchists, I wouldn't know.

There was a long theremin solo, which sounded slightly like a little girl soprano and slightly like the inside of a lemon. The drums beat in a Rite of Spring kind of rumble. I drank some more whiskey.

I didn't understand why it was so hard to find Sylvia. Usually people had so many ties, so many strings to follow. She was strangely untied. I'd emailed and called so many people. Some of them called back. Some of them knew her, but none of them knew where she was. None of them seemed concerned. Being alone at the bar, I felt untied too, unmoored like on the boat. No one knew where I was, nor cared. I felt the sensation of a person who had gone on a trip without telling anyone. It was an unhinged feeling, free but terrifying. If I just disappeared, who would know?

I thought about how all the intentional communities in the mid-nineteenth century tried to find freedom by changing our sexual relationships. They promoted free love or, like the Shakers, prohibited sex entirely. There was group parenting or no parenting. There was polygamy or no marriage. They tried anything to revise the idea of two married people raising their own children because, they reasoned, the basic structures of intimacy and love were also the basic structures of ownership. Sylvia's commune had done this, and now, maybe, she was doing it again in her way. Maybe Sylvia didn't want to be owned or to own anything or anyone. She wanted to be totally alone, unencumbered by society, free.

After the show, I went to the weekly dance party at a hip Moroccan restaurant. I'm not sure why I went. It was late. I was tired. My shin was still killing me. But I suppose some part of me was hoping it would be therapeutic. I remembered the anarchists dancing on the boat, jumping freely. It was the thing I most admired about them, more than their political schemes or their endless negotiations. Dancing might be what I needed. Dancing would be a way to access some self-centered bliss. I had this idea about dancing—that it could be some ritual of release, that it could be some purely physical, anti-intellectual activity outside any real economy or endgame that could take my mind off Sylvia. But I didn't really feel comfortable dancing, even when my shin was fine. Dancing always made me see myself with someone else's eyes, eyes of scorn. Dancing made me feel my failures.

So I sat at the bar and drank. The music was classic soul or eighties New Wave. There were, as usual, a lot of women there, beautiful women, fully involved in the physical transposition of their separate selves. I took a long sip of my beer. It occurred to me, as I was doing so, that I was probably already drunk, and this idea, as usual, was immediately denied by some devilish part of my brain that insisted that I wasn't. I was lucid, this part of me insisted. Everybody thinks they're lucid and sober and smart, just as everybody thinks they're sane. And maybe we are all sane in our ways. I kept drinking. I drank as if my throat needed immediate lubrication or it would never function again. Was I just trying to forget something?

"Did she drive you to drink?" Sylvia had asked me during our night together. Was she talking about Magda? Had I mentioned Magda?

When I looked up from this long, unnecessary, gratuitous draft of mediocre beer, I saw Agnes. I saw her red hair first, of course, that way she wore it, swooped back and curled around her face like Rita Hayworth in *Gilda*. She was unmistakable. I saw the skin of her cheek and I felt brighter. I would go talk to her; that's what I needed, I thought, and only then, after half-consciously musing about this, did I see her kiss a man. She was dancing with him over by the bay windows to a Prince song, dancing close, "I Wanna Be Your Lover," I think it was. You might call it dirty dancing. The man was pale and thin. His dark hair obscured her for a moment. Then she turned. She spun him. He was like a rag doll. She pulled him close again and grabbed his neck and kissed him, tongue first. I went toward her, getting up from my barstool, but immediately on seeing this tongue, this lizard-like addendum, I came to my senses and stopped. I was stuck there, torn between outrage and jealousy, and disgust at myself and titillation. But this was met by a new wave of revulsion as I looked at the boy's thick black hair and thin neck and realized it was Davis, the actor who had told me about his radical puppet show the night Sylvia took me to the supper club and then disappeared. Now I wanted to say, "Fuck your puppet show. That sounds stupid and pretentious." But I also wanted to ask him if he'd heard from Sylvia.

I did ask him. After the next song, they came to the bar and I caught their attention. They stood by my stool and we chatted about the music and about our apartments. Typical New York small talk. It was Agnes who brought up Sylvia first. Had I heard from her? No. Neither had she. Davis said, "Sylvia, Sylvia, Sylvia," in a singsong that was supposed to mean something, but I didn't know what.

"You haven't seen her either?" I said, just to put him on record.

"Nope," he said, making a goofy face.

"Agnes," I said next, "where did you hear that those guys at the market are selling Oxy?"

"From Sylvia," she said, turning to Davis. "Remember her story about those guys?"

"What guys?" he said. Now straight-faced.

"The guy with the beard and that young Latino guy, the hot one," she said. "They work with her at the farmers market."

"I don't know what you're talking about."

"Oxy," she said. "They get it from some New Age evangelist in Jersey. I swear you were there when she told me."

He furrowed his eyebrows, then raised them wide. "Oh, no, you mean the guys from my gym! That was *my* story. Chauncey and that weaselly guy Joel. They have the guru."

Davis took a drink and then launched into a story about a rich guy named Chauncey who seemed really nice but had all these strange secrets. He was selling OxyContin and raising rare snakes in his apartment, and he ran a newsletter about superconductors. That was the strangest part. The superconductors. Agnes apologized. Maybe she had gotten her stories confused. She could swear there was some story about the New Egypt guys that Sylvia had told.

"Blackwater?" I asked. They both looked at me like I was an idiot. They were probably right.

# Chapter 29

# THE DEFINITION OF SHORT

When you begin fact-checking, you are taught to underline everything in the text that is a verifiable fact, everything that is not "opinion." You use different colored pencils to organize your sources and topics. On my "Mandeville/Green" galleys, for example, I had underlined all the quotes and information that came from Jack Jarvis in red and all the background about the Greenmarket in green. I had underlined quotes or facts from other sources, like Sylvia, in blue. A few things were underlined in two colors because they might be checked in more than one way, or should be cross-checked. As I verified facts, I crossed them out word by word—or, in the case of proper nouns, letter by letter—to ensure the spelling was correct. I boxed a few sentences here and there, drawing a line to a box in the margins with comments. The margins on our galleys take up most of the page with a single thin column of text running down the middle, so that we have plenty of room on either side for comments and for edits. For "Mandeville/Green," though, my galleys were pretty clean. I'd crossed off just about everything. My comments were minimal. My corrections few.

I went through them all with Mandeville when he finally called me back on Wednesday. He apologized repeatedly about all our missed connections. He had been back with the homesteaders, where there was no reception. I only had a few more changes to go over, I said, so it would be quick. The River Garden flower farm was actually in Catskill, New York, not Hudson. Tom Poole was thirty-seven years old, not thirty-five, and he wasn't that "short" unless you call five feet ten short. And then there was the impression of the booming business of small farms, which wasn't exactly borne out by the economic figures. I had prepared a few fixes for that, some caveats. He was OK with most of them. We were basically done with the piece, but we still needed to edit a line about baked goods at the farmers market. I told Mandeville about the complex rules the Council on the Environment of New York City has. You don't have to source everything regionally, as he had written, but you need to score four points on a chart of localist practices. Then I suggested that we change a sentence about nightshades that was misleading. He was fine with that.

"I guess the only thing left," I said at last, "is this quote from Sylvia at New Egypt about 'nefarious business' at the farmers market."

"Did you speak with her?" Mandeville asked.

"Yes, I spoke to her, but—"

"Did you ask her about it?"

"I did," I said, "but she kind of dodged the question."

"She didn't deny saying it?"

"No. But she wants it removed from the piece. She said she doesn't want to be in there."

"So she knows it's in the piece and doesn't deny it?"

"Yes."

"Great. Then we're good, right? There shouldn't be any problem. We don't even name her."

Mandeville was right. We were good. We could run the quote. I should just check it off.

"It's just—she's kind of disappeared on me," I said. "She said she was worried about something at the farm, and she was supposed to call me back, but I don't know: something's worrying me."

"Ah—she's playing hard to get," he said, laughing. "I knew you'd like Sylvia."

"No one at the farm has seen her either," I said. It sounded strange coming out of my mouth, like I was lying or making more out of it than I should have been. I felt childish.

"Look," he said, "in my experience, if a girl doesn't call you back, she's not interested, or not interested enough to warrant a lot of second-guessing. There are lots of fish in the sea."

I felt a little sick. I didn't like the way Mandeville reduced people or changed the subject or turned me into a subject, a typical man, although he was probably more right than I wanted to admit. I had been on a date with Sylvia, she had needed a place to stay, maybe she had needed more than that, but we were drunk, and when she sobered up, she realized she wasn't interested. She was avoiding me. It was probably as simple as that. She didn't want to tell me directly, "I'm not interested." No one wanted to do that. Sure, she had come on to me, and maybe she flirted with the idea of seeing me again, but something had changed her mind, probably another man, I thought. That's why she left the farm. Sylvia was probably in an on-again, off-again relationship with someone. So many people fell into these relationships, as I had with Magda. Now we were off again, for good. But Sylvia was back on again, I guessed. I'd seen a recurring name in my background checks: Chistopher Conte. He was the artist who made "environmental installations." Maybe he was the religious guy she couldn't resist. He hadn't replied to my email inquiry. In any case, Mandeville was right. I didn't need to worry about her quote.

"Do you know if anyone sells drugs at the market?" I asked. "Oxy?"

"OxyContin?" Mandeville said.

"Yeah. I heard a rumor," I said, "about some guys selling out of the New Egypt stand."

He cleared his throat. "No," he said. "I never heard that."

He hadn't heard that. It was actually Davis and Chauncey from the gym. What else could I say? Had he seen any prostitutes at the market? Or anarchists?

"Thanks," I said.

"No, thank *you*," Mandeville said in his sensitive voice. "It's always a pleasure working with you."

Just before hanging up, he added, "Don't worry about that Sylvia quote. She's not really accusing anyone of anything, and besides, I've got it in my notes.

"Trust me," he said.


*Trust me.* I didn't trust Mandeville. I don't trust anyone, not completely. You might say I have "trust issues." I'm pretty sure Magda said that more than once. But doesn't everyone have trust issues? It would be crazy not to. Even our closest confidants, even our lovers, don't tell the whole truth and nothing but the truth all the time, not because they are liars or cheaters but because they are humans. They can't see everything or know everything. They have access only to a little bit of the truth, often a distorted bit. And then we have to weigh all these little bits. I didn't trust Mandeville, but I didn't trust Agnes either. Or that actor, Davis. I certainly didn't trust Jarvis. And I wasn't sure I trusted Sylvia. Hadn't she acted in all sorts of mysterious ways? She'd never been straightforward. Besides, Mandeville was right, even if he wasn't entirely trustworthy: The quote in the piece was fine. No one would worry about it. No one would notice. Honestly, I really didn't trust myself.

In the end I had to trust Mandeville provisionally. I had to move on from "Mandeville/Green." I turned in my checking proof.

Case closed.

# Chapter 30
# MULBERRY TREES

America has always been a place to imagine a New World, an Eden. Before the Civil War, as industrialism and slavery metastasized, more than one hundred thousand Americans tried out alternative, communitarian lifestyles in Shaker villages and Fourier phalanxes and the like. One of the utopian dreamers was the Marquis de Lafayette, whose statue I was looking at in Union Square the Saturday morning after "Mandeville/Green" had gone to press. I was no longer there on some half-cocked stakeout. But there I was all the same. Just enjoying the park and its memorials. I wasn't looking for any "nefarious business" or tracking down a woman I had met briefly. I wasn't worrying that some desire, some hope, had been squashed before I could even tell what I was hoping for. I was just thinking about Lafayette, who in 1827, the same year Robert Owen's socialist New Harmony was dissolved, founded his own idealistic agricultural community in Florida. At the time Lafayette was a hero in the United States. When he visited the States in 1823, the public came out in droves to welcome him. They named Fayetteville, North Carolina, after him, and gave him $200,000 and a land grant near Jacksonville. Lafayette was also an abolitionist. When he came here to New York, he toured the African Free School on Mulberry Street, and through most of America he traveled with the abolitionist and feminist Fanny Wright. Three years later when he launched his Florida commune, he did so with political aims. There, free white laborers would show the South that slavery was unnecessary. He planned for vineyards and olive groves and mulberry trees. The latter would apparently spark the silk trade in the Southern states. The laborers, mostly peasants from Normandy, arrived soon after, and immediately found it impossible to grow these things in the Panhandle. It wasn't the Mediterranean; it was a swamp. The vineyard failed before the season was through, and the Frenchmen scattered.

I liked the Lafayette statue all the same. It was sculpted by Frédéric-Auguste Bartholdi in 1871 and, like Bartholdi's Statue of Liberty, was a gift from France. Lafayette's hair curls into points like a tricorn hat. He has an open stance. One arm is draped in a flowing cape and extends toward the viewer. The other holds a sword to his heart. I liked many of the monuments in the park, even if no one paid them any mind. There was a huge equestrian statue of George Washington and a monumental bronze Lincoln—and, in the southwest corner of the park, that skinny statue of Gandhi, walking with a stick, tilting forward headfirst, heading toward the Barnes & Noble or maybe Staples. I felt slightly embarrassed that the statue reminded me of Ben Kingsley, who played Gandhi, more than it reminded me of Gandhi himself. I suppose the image of Gandhi from the film was more firmly entrenched in my mind than any images from newspapers or documentary footage. I knew little of Gandhi's real life. I felt then that I had a strange colonial or post-colonial impression of Gandhi, a mix of bad media and fictions, now manifested in this funny tilting statue. There was the plaque farther north that marked a row of linden tress planted to commemorate the Armenian Genocide. I knew that this word on the plaque, *genocide*, was a controversial one. Turkey still denies it. So many people still suffer over it. It was a poetic memorial, just trees. It was simple and could mean so much in so many different ways down the years.

As I circled the park that day, I thought the people should pay more attention to these memorials, that they should know about Lafayette and about our many fickle versions of heroism and our failed attempts to change the world, and they should know about Sylvia and all the farmers and any nefarious practices that might be clinging to their noble pursuits. But the people didn't notice Lafayette or Gandhi or the Armenian Grove; they were talking wildly as if into telephones, talking to God, I imagined. Others were in charge of children, struggling for shade, already overwhelmed by the August heat and by the stress of the day and the difficulties of being nannies for some absent parents who weren't paying Lafayette any mind either. Others maybe were buying OxyContin or seeking out prostitutes or johns. I couldn't tell. My desire that they should consider Lafayette, I thought, was moralistic and unreasonable, and maybe just stupid. Just like my pursuit of Sylvia. Plus, my shin still hurt, and I was perpetually hungover.

I walked to the north side of the park and bought some cherry tomatoes and garlic greens from Nick, a baguette from Bread Alone, and some zinnias from the flower girl. Nick and I talked baseball for a while. The flower girl told me about how much she liked tea. No one had seen Sylvia for three weeks.

\*   \*   \*

Just then my phone rang. It was Mandeville. This was strange. Mandeville had never called me on my cell phone before, certainly not on a Saturday afternoon. And "Mandeville/Green" had already gone to press. His voice sounded odd, not his familiar poet's voice, but a jittery voice.

"Are you free?" he asked, trying to sound casual.

I was free. Or as free as anyone is.

# Chapter 31

# 0 = NOT KNOWN

I was slightly anxious when I arrived at the Soho building. I had a romanticized image of Mandeville's loft based on rumors about celebrities and the downtown art scene, so approaching it didn't just make me uncomfortable in the same way that approaching any stranger's home did. It also spurred in me the awkward self-consciousness of the aspiring youngster in the great man's home, even though Mandeville and I were about the same age, or maybe because we were the same age but he'd written several books and countless articles and traveled in elite and glamorous circles. I felt some inchoate desire for something that, on closer inspection, I didn't really want. But perhaps I was just confusing my desires and my disdain. I was still annoyed by what Mandeville had said about "the girls" and about "playing hard to get," and I couldn't repress the thought that this strange call and strange voice had something to do with Sylvia, even though "Mandeville/Green" had already shipped to the printers. It was about to appear on newsstands and in mailboxes. My work was done. "I know Mandy," she had said when I first met her. "Terrible cook." Perhaps Mandeville was hiding something, and now he realized it wasn't worth hiding, or that he couldn't hide it anymore. Something terrible had happened to Sylvia. Or maybe I was just suffering from simple social anxiety. I hated entering other people's homes.

The loft was bright. That was the first thing I noticed, even before I noticed the many paintings, including what looked like a Rothko and a Jasper Johns, and before I noticed coolers, six or eight red coolers, the kind you'd take tailgating, along the walls. On the far left wall was a block of casement windows through which the sun poured across the wide-planked wood floors and across the only piece of furniture in the enormous room, a modern red sofa. It sat alone in the center.

"They're for extra meat," Mandeville said. He was talking about the coolers. "Sometimes there isn't enough space." He popped one open to show me. "Alligator," he announced. I looked up at him. "I have so much damn alligator meat," he said. "You want some? I mean, I don't know what to do with it all. I'm sick of it." He smiled a sort-of childish smile. "But they're sure fun to kill, alligators. It's like killing a monster."

"Shhh," he said, "I think the girls are sleeping." He led me into a hallway. "She's in here."

"Who's in here?" I asked.

"The lamb," Mandeville said.

"The lamb?"

"Well, maybe she's a sheep. She's sixteen months old, which is sort of old for a lamb. Derrick kept calling her a tween."

Mandeville opened the door to the bathroom. It was a long, narrow room. A piece of plastic sheeting covered the mosaic tile. It was an elegant bathroom. There was a big wooden tub and a soapstone sink, one of those peculiar modern luxuries that allude to a time before indoor plumbing. Huddled beneath it was a sheep. I recoiled

instinctively. I didn't feel comfortable in the presence of nondomesticated animals in domestic spaces. Come to think of it, I didn't really
feel comfortable with nondomesticated animals, period. Maybe not
domesticated animals either. This was especially weird, a sheep in an
apartment bathroom, or maybe a lamb in an apartment bathroom,
bleating. It was white in places, and also ash-gray. Dirty white. I saw
it breathing quickly. I looked at it closer, and its fur reminded me of
bichon frise dogs. I dated a girl in high school who had those dogs.
They were nervous, disgusting dogs. I never liked their skin, which you
could see through the patches of dirty white fur. It was a seemingly
translucent gray skin that was always pulsing with the nervous beat
of their tiny hearts. The worst part was that whenever I visited that
girlfriend's house—it was a beautiful, cold mansion—I felt just like the
dogs, a bald beating thing. And now, faced with a sheep in an elegant
New York apartment bathroom, I felt that way again, a bald beating
thing, next to a bald, bleating sheep. I had backed up against the door
while Mandeville walked toward the tub. He inspected some liquid on
the plastic sheeting. "She must have peed," Mandeville said. He looked
confused for a minute. Then he collected himself and smiled at me.

"Isn't she a beauty?" he said. "Hello, girl. Hello." He used
his poet's voice. He had lost it there for a while. But he conjured
it again. "She's a sweet little thing," he said, sounding almost like
Garrison Keillor. He reached toward the sheep. It tried to back up,
and it stumbled.

Mandeville turned away again and started wrapping up the wet
plastic sheeting. "Isn't she a beauty?" he said again without looking at
her. "Derrick saved her for me. I was going to go out to the farm and
he was going to show me how to slaughter her. We had the whole
thing planned for the piece I'm writing on homesteading, but then the

weather wouldn't cooperate, and rescheduling was difficult. I had to go to Biarritz—Zora is shooting there—and then with the girls, well . . . Finally, I just figured, I'll do it at home. It'll make a great story." Mandeville had wrapped up the wet plastic awkwardly, trying not to soil his clothes. I was still against the door. "Look, isn't she a beauty?" he said, and again turned his well-groomed salt-and-pepper stubble toward the sheep. He laid the plastic in the tub. He approached the animal, which still cowered under the sink and was nervously bleating. Mandeville dropped to his knees awkwardly. One knee fell into a wet spot. Urine. The lamb skittered back. Mandeville reached out to pet it. It flailed and slipped again. It clearly wasn't used to tile floors. Mandeville said, with deep empathy, "You're a good little girl," as he grabbed hold of her neck. "Look," he said, turning to me, "she's so soft." I had slightly adjusted to the situation and now the anxiety that had been purely physical at first had become more conscious. There was a shivering lamb in the bathroom with me, and now I knew we were going to kill it.

"You've never done this before?" I asked him. We were sitting in his office adjacent to the bathroom.

"I've seen it done," he said, "plenty of times. But I never did it myself."

I nodded in a way that I hoped was more sympathetic than judgmental, although I thought, You idiot! Who brings home a sheep to a house while his wife and child are sleeping? Who brings home a lamb to kill in their fancy Soho loft by the soapstone sink and a Japanese soaking tub and doesn't even know how to kill it?

"I thought you might help me," he said, "make sure we do it right."

So that's why Mandeville had called me on a Saturday. He didn't know how to kill his sheep and he thought I might help him research it. I took this as a compliment, even as I wanted no part in the killing. I thought, Perhaps Mandeville respects me; he admires my careful and thorough approach to problem-solving. Or perhaps he just wants a servant, a discreet servant. He knew I would be tactful. Or maybe he knew I'd be curious, which I was, despite my visceral revulsion to the sheep and to the idea of killing it. Now that I knew about it, I had to know more. I had to find out how to kill it, and besides, I eat meat. I'd had lamb twice recently, a lamb with rice dish from a food cart and shepherd's pie from St. Dymphna's. Hadn't I just been thinking that meat eaters should be involved, at least once, in the killing of that meat? We shouldn't just distance ourselves in our corridors of doom and let the meat come wrapped up and prepared with no sign of where it came from or how it got there or what creature gave its life to feed us. Someone had killed that lamb I'd eaten. I should understand the killing, the sacrifice, or so I told myself. What would Sylvia do? Worship the Deity. I said nothing to Mandeville. We prepared for the slaughter.

The problem was that most sources expected that you would use a shotgun to kill your lamb, and Mandeville wasn't going to do that in his apartment bathroom. He showed me some of his homesteading books, and I got an overview of the shotgun method. I read that often you'd give the lamb little to eat the night before, just some water and some hay. This would make disemboweling less messy and also make it easy to get the lamb to duck its head. You just put some feed in front of it, and when it ducks down, place the shotgun about six to eight inches from the back of the head, between the eyes, aiming down in line with the neck. Drawings showed the line of fire that will most quickly and painlessly rid the sheep of its last breath.

"I've read all this stuff," said Mandeville. "None of it tells you how to kill it without a gun."

I put down the books in the pile on Mandeville's desk and started searching on his computer. I didn't trust many of the initial sources I was finding on the web, so I went deeper. I logged onto LexisNexis with my work password and searched through various journals and periodicals. I finally found and printed out two things: a guide for New Zealand sheep farmers and an academic paper from Colorado State University about the differences between kosher and halal humane killing of sheep. The New Zealand guide listed many different techniques for killing, including a swift blow to the head. It had diagrams and helpful hints. The academic paper concentrated on knives and knife techniques. The key was in the sharpness of the knife. It must be very, very sharp—there were all kinds of regulations cited—to qualify as humane slaughter. The article suggested this: "To test the knife it should be able to slice a standard A4 printer paper that is held dangling by one corner. The knife must be dry for this test." Why paper, and why particularly A4 paper? It almost seemed as if they were plotting a slaughter in the office. I looked up A4. I had to poke around for a while, but eventually I found the website for ISO, the International Organization for Standardization, a body interested in standardizing everything. They had a standard for brewing tea, and a standard for "language-neutral" representation of the human sexes: 0 = not known, 1 = male, 2 = female, 9 = not applicable. The ISO had invented the "A" paper sizes with the aspect ratio of $1:\sqrt{2}$. A4 was 8.3 by 11.7 inches. I figured 8.5 by 11 inches would do. I got some paper and Mandeville chose a knife. "It must be," I read to him, "at least six inches or long enough that the tip of the blade would remain outside the edge of the neck." Mandeville had a fabulously outfitted kitchen with just about every killing device you can imagine, so we had a lot of choices. We settled on an eight-inch Japanese-style Misono knife. It was razor-sharp, he said. I gave a piece of paper to Mandeville. He held it up and sliced. His motion blew the paper sideways, and the knife completely missed. I considered a joke about how that wasn't going to cut it, but I refrained. I could see that Mandeville was nervous. He sliced again. This time the paper made that incisive noise and two-thirds of the sheet fluttered away from Mandeville's hand down onto the parquet floor.

"We are going to have to hang it up to bleed as soon as the killing is done," I told Mandeville as I looked through my printouts. "Is there a place to hang it?"

"Yes," he said. "I was thinking we could use the chin-up bar in my study. We can mount it above the tub."

Mandeville went down to the basement to get a drill. I returned to the computer. I started looking through Mandeville's email. I searched for "Sylvia." I found a series of spam emails from someone named Miss Sylvia Dominique: "Greetings," one of them began, "it is my pleasure contacting you to make this noble request. I expect you're not going to let down this trust I am about to repose on you; for the fact that we have not yet known or written to each other before. Though I will not compel you to honor this request, against your will." Back to my search results, I scrolled down to a back-and-forth series of emails between Mandeville and someone named Caroline Liu about a massage appointment Mandeville had missed and then

apologized for and rescheduled. The emails were full of sexual innuendo. Mandeville said, "I'm looking for the ultimate release." Liu
responded that he would feel "a rush through every part of his body,
every part," she repeated. Maybe this wasn't innuendo. I couldn't be
sure. In any case, it wasn't helping me find Sylvia or feel better about
the sheep. I thought about it again, locked in the bathroom, far from
home, a bald beating thing. I felt a little sick. I'd never killed anything.
I mean, I'd killed the occasional fly or cockroach, and once when I was
a child I killed some frogs accidentally, thinking I was performing an
important experiment by launching them in a water balloon shooter.
I guess I'd killed some mice too in traps. But nothing this big, nothing
so close in scale to humans, nothing so full of blood.

All this time I was going along with Mandeville's terrible plan. I
hadn't mentioned Sylvia or the Greenmarket story. There was nothing to mention. The story had gone to press. I searched Mandeville's
email for "tomato." I came up with a few different exchanges with
Jack Jarvis and a few with me. I opened an old Jarvis email from
right around the time I'd met Sylvia. It was filled with weird Jarvis-
like nonsense about the independent nature of tomatoes. "It's like
Steiner said," Jarvis wrote. "Tomatoes have no desire to step outside
of themselves, no desire to step outside the realm of strong vitality.
That's where they want to stay. They are the least social beings in
the entire plant kingdom. They do not want anything from strangers,
and above all, they do not want any fertilizer that has gone through a
composting process; they reject all that. This is the reason that they
can influence what works independently within the human or animal
organism. They are masters of independence." I wasn't sure exactly
what he meant but it sounded like bullshit. Jarvis probably thought

of himself as a radical individualist and had some crackpot botanical theories to justify himself. He was an egoist. Eat tomatoes and rely on yourself, he seemed to be saying. Don't be a pussy, pussy.

I scanned through a few more emails till I found a reference, right around the time that Sylvia had called me, to "the hot tomato." "Having problems down here with the hot tomato," Jarvis wrote. "Has she spoken to you? She's got her panties in a bunch." That was the phrase he used, *panties in a bunch*. At the end of the email, after running through a few other pieces of news, Jarvis mentioned again: "And if the tomato calls, don't listen to her. I don't know what's gotten into her," he wrote, and then added, "And re: your question. Don't worry. I've got you covered. I can get you whatever you want. Many thanks, Jack." I scrolled up looking for the question.

Mandeville walked in. I felt like I was caught doing something illicit, although maybe I was catching *him* doing something illicit. It didn't matter. I had that jittery feeling one gets when one has done something wrong and does not want anyone to know but suspects, irrationally, that everyone knows, that everyone is watching and judging. Mandeville had the drill and the chin-up bar. He raised his eyebrows. I stumbled out of his chair and murmured something. He headed for the bathroom. I followed. We inspected the wall above the soaking tub. It was drywall. I tried to turn a screw into it. It just crumbled. The sheep was still under the sink, a huddled, little, dirty thing. Mandeville went over to pet it nervously every few minutes. We tried one of those yellow stud finders on the wall to look for some wood to anchor the screws, but the lights on the stud finder, which were supposed to switch on when passing over a beam, kept blinking wildly, and neither of us could interpret this properly, nor were we convinced when we knocked on various places whether the sound was right. I thought Mandeville was treating me strangely. He was onto me. Or I was onto him. But maybe it was just a strange situation. We decided to use the big drywall anchors, those metal toggle devices that spring open inside the wall like some kind of medieval weapon. We had to drill a large hole to squeeze this torture device through. While I was measuring for drilling locations, I thought I should ask Mandeville about the emails. He was in some conspiracy with Jarvis, I thought; that's what Jarvis was suggesting when he said he'd get him anything he wanted. Jarvis was saying, "I'll take care of you; just keep your mouth shut," or maybe, "just shield your eyes." Perhaps Mandeville didn't know what Jarvis was up to, but he suspected something. Perhaps he'd rather not find out: He didn't want to ruin his story; it was a good story. But Sylvia had found out, and she wasn't like Mandeville. She couldn't be a part of it, so she had fled, skipped town, or worse. She'd been "taken care of." I thought of the ponytailed guy I saw at the market. "Don't worry, it's done," he had said. "Problem solved. The murder is done. I won't say how or who did it; it just happened." But the ponytailed guy wasn't talking about murder, and no one had killed Sylvia. I looked back at the lamb. It was calm now, just sitting under the sink, waiting to die. I drilled a hole. The sound of the drill made the sheep jump and push hard against the wall like an autistic child who must be pressed or squeezed hard to feel safe. "It's got to be bigger," Mandeville kept saying as he tried to force the anchor through. I changed the drill bit from five-sixteenths to three-eighths to one-half, the biggest we had, and then I jiggled it around to make it even bigger. Mandeville got it. We did three more and fastened the bar. "Try it," I said. He pulled himself up, bending his long legs to dangle above the tub. The bar held, I looked at the cracked Sheetrock in the bottom of the Japanese soaking tub. We'd already done some serious damage, but the lamb was still alive.

I stood beside the tub while Mandeville climbed in, carrying the sheep with him. Mandeville had changed into white painter's pants that seemed almost carefully smudged with a variety of colors, mostly melon red and a medium beige. He was wearing a white scoop-neck T-shirt too. The outfit gave him the look of an artist from another time period, like Picasso was hoisting this lamb or sheep or tween animal into the elegant wooden Japanese soaking tub, a thin young Picasso with slicked-back hair. The sides of the tub were high, and Mandeville struggled a bit. I tried to help by grabbing the back legs of the sheep to fold them up and over the edge, but as I leaned toward the animal, Mandeville heaved it up again and I stumbled into man and sheep both, nearly knocking them over. In the end this bungling actually did the trick. Man and sheep were in the tub. The sheep for its part didn't seem to mind. It was relaxed again. Mandeville was still holding it and petting its side and whispering into its ear sweet nothings in his soft and breathy poet's voice.

We had gone over the script a few times and studied the diagrams because the actual killing had to be quite quick and precise. I read it again aloud. "'Restrain the sheep gently but firmly,'" I told Mandeville, "'standing or lying on its left side with its chin in your left hand (vice versa if left-handed), to extend the neck. Part the wool over the throat just behind the angle of the jaw. Make a swift firm cut across the upper part of the neck, severing the carotid arteries and both jugular veins. The trachea and esophagus will also be severed. It must be one quick, deep slice through all of these things,'" I told him again, "'or the animal will not die instantly and will struggle in pain. A huge amount of blood will be seen pumping from the arteries,'" I read, "'so be warned if you don't like the sight of blood! And be careful not to drop the knife.' It says that many people, shocked at the blood, cut their legs when the knife slips out of their hand."

"Don't worry," said Mandeville. "We'll be all right," he said gently to the sheep.

"'You will know the sheep is dead,'" I said, "'as opposed to unconsciousness, when the eye pupils are widely distended, and there is no blinking reflex when the surface of the eye is touched. And of course, there will be no pulse, and it will stop breathing,'" I read. "'The sheep should die in three to eight seconds,'" I said, "'and you should hold it firmly until then.'

"Three to eight seconds," I said again. "Isn't that kind of a big gap? It's a bit too precise without being precise at all, don't you think?" Mandeville laughed. I laughed too. It was a nervous laugh. Three to eight seconds. I counted it out in my head, one one-thousand, two one-thousand, three one-thousand, and so on.

Mandeville whispered to the lamb, "You're a good little girl, such a good little girl." Six one-thousand, seven one-thousand. It seemed like an eternity.

"Should I get the knife?" I asked. We had left it outside the room. I don't think either of us wanted the sheep to see it, as if it might then know what was going to happen and panic. Mandeville nodded.

"You're a good little girl," he said. I got the knife and a large silver mixing bowl. I would use it to catch the blood.

Mandeville made the cut. He seemed shaky at first, but then he almost seemed to go into a trance, whispering something unintelligible in the blond wood Japanese soaking tub. He breathed slowly, but it looked difficult, to muscle the knife through all that hair and flesh. He seemed to cut almost too deep, halfway through the neck. The knife stuck, and Mandeville tensed. The lamb bucked. Mandeville grabbed it harder and ripped the knife viciously through the rest of the neck. One one-thousand. Two one-thousand. It kicked. It convulsed. It kicked again. The blood came. I haven't seen blood like that. Ever. It was pumping like a geyser straight from the neck in irregular bursts. Pump. Pump. Pump. The heart struggling to squeeze that blood for the sake of recovery when all it was doing was killing itself squeezing that blood out into the silver bowl that I could barely hold. It squirted across that gray-white fur and across my jelly arms and across Mandeville's white painter's pants and into the tub. It wasn't the amount of blood; it was the motion and the thickness and the never-ending spurting of it and the color, and also it *was* the amount. A ton of blood. Three one-thousand, four one-thousand—I tried to calm myself. I couldn't. I dropped the bowl. It clattered on the wooden tub, splattering blood. The sheep kicked. I held the end of the tub to keep from falling. Five one-thousand. Six one-thousand. I slipped into a dream state. I saw the blood and the fur as a machine or a movie, or something very far away and strange. I was dispassionately curious now, holding on to the edge of the tub. How long would the machine run? How long could it pump? Seven one-thousand. Eight one-thousand.

It ended. The sheep slumped. Its head was now like a flap folded away from the neck. In place of the face was a splotchy mushroomy red pulp. Mandeville still held on, slumped over the sheep, breathing heavily. I took the knife from him and put it in the sink with the bowl, which was still mostly full of blood. We didn't speak.

Mandeville grabbed the hind legs and tied a complicated knot around them with the rope, and then tied another one for good measure. It was gnarly, but it held. He ducked under the sheep and pulled it up on top of his back, where it hung like a child or a cape. It reminded me of a lion cape on a Hercules statue, but Mandeville wasn't built like Hercules; he was a young, lanky Hercules with carefully coiffed hair and a dead sheep on his back, a lanky, stooped Hercules in a Picasso painter's outfit in his blond Japanese soaking tub in his Soho loft. I pulled the rope up over the chin-up bar and dropped my hips to let my weight work with gravity. The sheep rose up. The bar held. The blood flowed. As we hung the sheep, I thought of all the lynchings that had taken place in Union Square. I didn't want to think this—I didn't want to compare the death of this animal to that of a human, especially a human murdered for some terrible reason—but there it was in my brain. The bloody, mushroom neck was the tortured flesh of a human, and I was the angel of death. I thought of the children's game hangman. What a strange, cruel game it was. I couldn't believe that I'd never really thought of it as cruel. I'd never thought about real hangings when I played the game hangman, I never thought of death, and now I feared I wouldn't be able *not* to think of it. He was hanged at 4:00. You use the past participle *hanged*, not *hung*, for humans, to distinguish this from, say, curtains, which are hung, not hanged. H-A-N-G-E-D. The sheep or lamb or tween was hanged. We tied it up and let it bleed.

# Chapter 32

# RUG AROUND HER

Mandeville stood at the marble countertop pouring us drinks. His summer whites, sweat-drenched and browned with blood, clung to his body. He was pouring clear liquid out of two unlabeled bottles. Apothecary bottles. "Russian military liquors," he said. "Got them from an elk hunter in the Taiga. We hunted on homemade skis. They're wonderful." He said *wonderful* with an exaggerated, singsongy first syllable. WUHn-der-ful. Like he hadn't just killed a sheep. Mandeville poured some on the rocks and lifted his glass. "To the tween," he said.

"The tween," I repeated. I took a big slug. The still-warm liquor churned in my stomach. It tasted of cough medicine. I thought of Sylvia. I imagined her hanged with blood running across her scarred face. I tried not to think of it, but there she was. My mind was going its own way. She's gone for a Burton and gone for a shit with a rug around her. I drank some more.

"Alligator stew?" Mandeville said. He took some Tupperware out and poured a rust-colored mush into two bowls. "I made this on Thursday," he said. "It gets better after a few days in the fridge." Mandeville slowly and carefully grated cheese on top, almost like he was following a recipe and measuring it out. He put a bowl in the microwave and then filled our glasses again, this time with a different liquor. "This one's made with nettles," he said, "very aromatic."

I knocked it back. Still cough medicine to me.

"She's dead," I said.

"Yep," said Mandeville. "Thank you so much for your help." He swirled his glass constantly as he talked. It was either affectation or OCD or both. "Now I have to skin her."

"I mean Sylvia," I said.

Mandeville looked confused. "Sylvia?" he said.

"I think something happened to her. She's completely disappeared."

He looked at me a minute. Then he laughed. "Still haven't heard anything from her?" he said, swirling his glass. "So you think she's in some kind of danger? You've got a hell of an imagination."

"*You* haven't heard anything?" I asked.

"Nothing. But why would I?" Mandeville said. "I'm sure she's fine. She's a—how do I say it—" He looked around conspiratorially, just as he had when he first told me about her. Then he looked right at me. "She's a free spirit," he said.

A free spirit? He seemed to be implying something more. Maybe he was saying she was a flake or a slut or both. Maybe he had slept with her, with "the hot tomato." I wondered how I might bring that up. It was probably an inside joke between Mandeville and Jarvis.

"Jarvis acted very weird and defensive about her," I said, "like they had a fight or she was making accusations about him. He seemed worried that she might tell me something. Did she find something incriminating?"

"Jarvis?" Mandeville swirled his glass and stroked his chin. "I wouldn't take too much stock in what he says. He has a"—he paused—"somewhat skewed version of reality. He's a bit of a paranoid, always acting like someone was out to get him. I had to constantly reassure him."

Mandeville gave me a look like was suddenly seeing me for the first time. "She really got her hooks into you, didn't she?" he said, laughing in a way that may have been mocking me or may have been an expression of genuine sympathy, or perhaps both. "If you want," he said, "I'll ask around about her. I'm sure we can track her down."

I nodded. "Thanks," I said. I knew he wouldn't track her down. With Mandeville, I always had to track things down myself. Phone numbers, people's names, ex-lovers. As soon as he said he'd look for something, I knew it was lost. And besides, Jarvis had Mandeville in his pocket. He was giving Mandeville "anything he needed" down at the farm. Maybe OxyContin, maybe something else.

"You've been down to New Egypt a few times, right?"

"Of course, of course," Mandeville said, as if I were accusing him of insufficient reporting.

"What's it like? What goes on there?"

"Just your average hippie bacchanal," Mandeville said, smiling and compulsively swirling his cough medicine. "Actually, it's pretty dull. Jarvis loves to lecture, and all the kids have to sit and listen to him and respond dutifully. It's like a boring academic cult."

The microwave dinged. Mandeville brought over the alligator stew.

"Are there a lot of drugs?"

Mandeville shrugged. "Just the usual," he said. "A joint around the campfire. That's not my thing. I'm a whiskey man." He watched me closely, swirling and drinking and swirling and drinking. Not whiskey.

"Sylvia didn't tell you about something illegal, something Jarvis was selling?" I asked. I swallowed a spoonful of stew. Before I really tasted it, it hit me. I put my hand over my mouth and scurried to the bathroom. Terrible cook, I heard Sylvia saying. I opened the door: The hanging sheep, now bloody, matted, and limp, trickling into the tub. I threw up in the soapstone sink.

# PART THREE
# UNKNOWN KNOWNS

# Chapter 33

# A GREAT BIG BARREL

The Garden State. No one knows where that nickname for New Jersey came from. I looked it up when I was checking "Mandeville/Green"—not that I had to; I was just curious. The *Encyclopedia of New Jersey* had nothing. After a bit more digging, I found some newspaper articles attributing the name to Abraham Browning, a prominent nineteenth-century lawyer who owned a farm in Camden. He supposedly gave a speech to the Centennial Exhibition in 1876 calling New Jersey a great big barrel full of good things to eat, open on both ends so that New Yorkers and Pennsylvanians could reach in and grab them. He called it the "Garden State," and according to the articles the name stuck. I wasn't satisfied with these reports, though. It looked like they were all derived from the same source, as is often the case. They all had almost identical language, including the sentence "he called it the Garden State, and the name has stuck ever since." The sentence was cribbed from Alfred Heston, an Atlantic City historian, and Heston wasn't very reliable. Abraham Browning certainly didn't come up with the open-ended-barrel image, as Heston suggested. That went back further, at least to Benjamin Franklin. It was a weird image too. It seemed odd that you'd brag about being a vessel for others, a kind of giving tree.

"The Garden State," I heard myself say out loud. I didn't realize I was speaking. It made me wonder what else I might have said that I had thought I had only thought.

Nick and I had been driving silently since dawn. The only sound was the constant, loud metallic rattle of Nick's beat-up step-van. We were headed to New Egypt Farms. I needed to go there, I decided, after I killed the lamb and read Mandeville's email exchange with Jarvis. I wasn't exactly panicked and paranoid like I had been in Mandeville's apartment, but there was something about the "panties in a bunch" comment that I couldn't shake. It's a disgusting, dismissive, antifeminist thing to say—and so visual. I couldn't get it out of my mind and couldn't rest without seeing the farm, to find out if Sylvia had discovered something there, to learn what "nefarious business" was going on and whether that "nefarious business" had driven Sylvia away, or if she was just avoiding me. Or not me. Something else. Someone else. Nick arranged the trip. It was perfect timing, he said. There was going to be a special seminar and a big bonfire that night. We left before six and had barely talked since.

"The Garden State," Nick repeated. "I've actually always liked that. It's quaint."

"When they put it on license plates back in 1954," I told him, "Governor Meyner actually vetoed the bill."

"Wasn't into gardening? Too much of an old lady thing?"

"Yeah. I think he wanted something more . . ." I said. "Something more industrial. All the farms were dying out at that time—"

"Fucking still are dying out—"

"Yeah, they still are dying out," I said. We both looked out at the industrial wasteland near the Meadowlands. We smelled it too, although I knew that rotting smell was likely from natural causes, plants decomposing in the marsh.

"I guess he was right, though, about the Garden State," Nick said. "Ain't no gardens around here." He took a deep, dramatic breath of the terrible air for effect. The word *ain't* rang in my ears. We had quoted Sylvia as saying, "It ain't all green." I'd always doubted that she would use that word, but Nick would. He did.

"It's more like the Heavy Metal State," Nick said.

We rumbled through the Heavy Metal State without talking. A young woman in a Toyota passed us. Nick hit the gas. The van shook but didn't catch her. I watched her Garden State plates recede into the distance. Nick must have been watching the plates too because he blurted, "License plates are bullshit anyway. Classic example of government overreach."

"Overreach?" I said. "You don't think they help keep the roads safe?"

"You've been to the DMV, right?" Nick continued. "It's like a big fat fucking argument for libertarianism, or any fucking shit other than the bullshit we've got. Jesus, last time I was there, I'm in line for, like, an hour and then the dude working is wearing an eye-patch, a fucking eye-patch, like he's Captain Hook. And guess what? He's a royal A-one dick. Fucker makes me go through the line again, another fucking forty minutes, 'cause I'm missing a fucking form that says I got my van as a gift, the special fucking gift form. No one wanted this fucking van. It was free. Fuh-ree. But free ain't free, dude. It's, like, illegal to get shit for free—unless you're George Fucking W. Fucking Bush. Then everything's fucking free of charge, dude, on a golden fucking platter," he said. He spit out the window.

"Nothing good comes out of the state," he said. "It's just eating its own shit."

"But look around," I said. We passed another dead factory. "This used to be—the earth. Don't we need to make sure we don't fuck it up even more?"

"Jesus fucking Christ, fact-checker. Government regulations aren't doing shit for this place. The state's not stopping pollution. Pollution is a dick they fuck you with. If you free the marketplace— and I'm talking about really fucking freeing it, dude, not some half-regulated, rigged bullshit system—you'll see. Shit's going to change. Nobody wants to breathe this. Only rich people who can jet off to Banff or some shit."

"Yeah, yeah," I said.

"Free your market. Free your mind," Nick said.

That was his mantra. Free your market. Free your mind. I didn't buy it. I couldn't even fathom a totally free exchange, free of politics and chemical weapons and greed, which I suppose was a failure (again) of my imagination. I had more faith in utopian socialism or anarchist collectives than in free markets, and I didn't have much faith in those. Even if I could imagine a totally free exchange, I didn't believe it would provide equity or morality or sanity. People buy and sell things for so many reasons. People buy and sell tomatoes bathed in chemicals and bred with tough skins to last forever. Tasteless tomatoes. They don't know any better. It's hard to know what you're buying when you buy something. It's hard to understand what choices have been made for us before we even have a choice. I didn't think a free market would fix this. It wouldn't magically reveal all. And besides, even when we do know better, even when we understand that a certain tomato is the fruit of an earth-killing system, showered in petrochemicals and diesel fumes, even then we might choose that bad tomato. People buy and sell terrible things. They buy and sell guns and drugs and women and children. Even at the farmers market—was it a free market? I wondered. It had so many rules. What kind of freedom were we talking about? Even there you could probably buy sex or drugs or both.

I looked at a long row of parking lots. The asphalt to our left had been retaken by a tangle of weeds. There was something quite beautiful about it, actually, especially after the smell died down and the blue light of dawn lingered. Nick stepped on the gas. My whole body rattled, but we barely sped up.

# Chapter 34

# THE ROMANCE OF LABOR

And then the landscape changed. It was quick. Even in a beat-up van that could barely hit fifty-five, we passed suddenly into the countryside. Small barns dotted the area along Monmouth Road. Tall pines alternated with combed fields of tall grass. It was jarring to make these transitions, so close to New York, in the most densely populated and terribly polluted state. Suddenly it was like we were in another country. New Jersey, I thought, Walt Whitman's state. It contained multitudes.

We skirted the Pine Barrens, cruising along flat roads under a flat sky held up by rows of lonely telephone poles. I thought of the Russian guy in the *Sopranos* episode who had to dig his own grave. It was probably nearby. I thought too about how Paulie says the Russian is an "interior decorator," not in the "interior ministry," and how weird, in the first place, it is to call something the "interior ministry." We pulled down a long dirt driveway somewhere near a town called Cream Ridge. The New Egypt Geodynamic Agricultural Institute wasn't actually in New Egypt. It was somewhere near Cream Ridge.

The farm was nothing like I expected. It wasn't old, not in any way. The farmhouse looked like a large suburban prefab home, a big rectangle with a peaked roof and shiny new siding. It was the kind of place where you might buy skis or discount liquor. There were a series of hoop houses beyond it. They were high-tech looking, huge, clean white, and plasticky. They reminded me of the movie *E.T.* when the scientists probe the alien, and I half thought, when I first encountered them, that I'd have to put on a complex space suit, the kind of suit the anarchists were going to wear at the RNC protest, and breathe through some creepy ventilator to enter. Overalls and a trucker hat wouldn't cut it. Even the tractor, which ran on biofuel, looked brand-new. A shiny, sleek yellow-and-green vehicle, it reminded me of a child's toy. But maybe this showed my ignorance. I'm not sure why I thought everything on a farm should be old, dirty, dilapidated. I hadn't seen that many tractors. I guess my farm images were all from old movies and Willie Nelson's Farm Aid, not from any real experience.

We dropped our stuff in the little prefab log cabin Nick shared with a guy called Per and walked back toward the main house. That's when I saw Jack Jarvis for the first time in person. Standing in the sun at the top of the hill as if he were waiting for us, as if he were watching our every move. Or maybe I was just paranoid. He didn't look very menacing. He was a short, gray-haired man in a pressed olive polo shirt and creased navy chinos, more like a middle manager on a golf outing than a hippie cult leader—or a farmer. Jack grabbed my hand firmly in his large wrinkled paw. He looked me right in the eye in a way that could be interpreted as solicitous or intimidating, depending on your inclination. I chose to be intimidated. "Damn glad you could come out here," he said in a slow drawl, "and see all these wonderful things we are doing." I noticed a hearing aid in his ear. I pulled my hand away. It was hot. That was what I felt, slightly hot, slightly uncomfortable, not drawn in by some deep charisma as many had been drawn in, but not driven away either, as perhaps Sylvia had been driven away, wherever she was. I did feel that I was in the presence of a macho man. I was in the presence of a jerk. I thought that right away.

"I'm so glad that Nick invited me out," I said.

"We all invite you," he said. "I hope you are coming to the development and staying the night."

"Yes, sir, I am," I said in the manner of a cadet.

"Nick," said Jarvis, "you make sure this young man has everything he needs." Jarvis's cowboy rhythms were slow and easy yet forceful. "He's an important man," Jarvis continued. Then he winked at me. I forced a smile.

I followed Nick around the immediate area of the barn and cabin. He explained what was what, what fields were growing things and which were fallow, and all the complexities of geodynamic farming, Jarvis's variation on Rudolf Steiner's biodynamics, but he did so in such a rapid and disorganized way, as he checked on the hay, grabbed the plastic mulch, began to spray things, and directed the interns this way and that way, that I got slightly lost. Now we were leaving the barn out of a different door than the one we entered by, I was fairly sure. We passed a greenhouse that I hadn't seen. Or maybe I had. At one point, we passed an Airstream trailer near the edge of the woods. Nick said the trailer was Jarvis's office. "Sort of a private man cave," he said. I looked up at the sun, still close to the horizon. We were heading southeast. That I could say for sure. The air was still early-morning crisp. It was the last weekend of August, and the grasses were wet with dew. You could smell it. I smelled it.

The next thing I knew I was digging. I had agreed to help with the potatoes, although I must admit I was somewhat disappointed with the job. I would rather have worked on something more alive, something greener. It was called the Greenmarket, after all, not the Brownmarket. From time to time I looked up at Melanie, who was overseeing the potato picking. Melanie was a pleasant-seeming woman in plaid and pigtails. She was very young, I thought at first, but then I wasn't exactly sure. I may have been fooled by her look, the cutoff jeans, the little-girl hair. She had a raspy voice and a leathery face. It was like she was a hard-drinking teenybopper. I wondered how hard the work of farming must be on the body. I was deep in the dirt at this point, fully immersed in dirt like a worm or a seedling. It was very brown work. Brown potatoes, brown earth. You don't dig potatoes until the potato plants are dead. I suppose everything we eat dies before we eat it, or just about everything. But I also knew the brown potato bulb had sucked all the green power of the plant and basically killed it. Potatoes were an afterlife, a ghost of something that was, a ghost of summer. I remembered the Irish famine memorial that I had visited with Agnes the night she told me that New Egypt vendors were selling Oxy. Potatoes were the ghosts of so many dead Irish people and suffering immigrants. All they could get were potatoes, and when the potatoes all died of blight, everything died.

I looked up at Raina, an aging volunteer. She seemed to be digging faster than I was. I took off my gloves, wiped my face, took a sip of water, and redoubled my efforts. I tried to dig quickly but not recklessly. I tried to improve my technique. I imagined what it might be like to do this every day, to do what you might call "real work," physical work. My uncle Mike would call it that. It's not fake work like sitting in an office and turning paper into trash, producing nothing. They both hurt your back, though, I thought, digging potatoes and sitting in a cubicle, but it's a different kind of pain. The novelty of physical labor would fade, I knew, after a few days or weeks on the farm. It would seem less romantic. But then I thought some part of it would always be romantic. Some part of working with your hands was indivisible. Digging in the earth, pulling out potatoes, not thinking. But you must think. You must worry. You must think about money and the impossibility of it, the tragedy of farming, the slave labor, the blight. Most people who dig potatoes are poor. Most of them suffer.

I took a sack over to Melanie, who was working near the truck, and I refilled my water. She glistened with sweat and smiled.

"Did you know Sylvia well?" I asked after a minute.

"Oh, yeah," she said. "We were buds. You a friend of hers?" She pulled off her gloves and fixed her pigtails. "I miss her," she said.

"Any idea what happened to her?" I asked in a way that I hoped was both pointed, as if I knew something, and open, as if it might be anything.

"Not really," she said. "I mean, she left a few weeks ago, just up and left. People said she went to South America or something, but I don't know. She didn't mention it to me." Melanie put some potatoes on the back of the truck. "It was kind of weird, but, you know, she was kind of"—Melanie paused and looked up at me—"private," she said.

I grabbed another sack of potatoes and threw it on the truck.

"Last time I talked to her," I said, "it seemed like something out here had spooked her, something on the farm." I lifted up another bag. "Like she saw something that bothered her," I said, throwing the bag on the truck, "and then she disappeared."

Melanie looked like she was going to say something. I waited. She didn't speak.

"Any idea," I finally asked, "what was bothering her?"

"I think—" Melanie began. She didn't look at me. She kept working. "Look, this may be just me," she said. "Don't tell anyone I said this, but, I think—" She hopped off the truck. The sun was brighter now and bearing down on us. "I think she had a crush on Jack, and he just wasn't into her."

"Jarvis?" I said. "That's funny. I got the impression that they didn't get along that well." I helped her lift another bag of potatoes. I sweated. She didn't say anything. "I got the impression," I said, "that maybe it was something Jack had done, or some secret he had—"

"Jack?" she said, cutting me off. "You don't know Jack." She turned away and went back to her dirt patch.

I packed up the last bags and thought how to reapproach the Sylvia questions. I drifted slightly toward Melanie and said, trying to sound curious: "Tell me about him, about Jack."

"What can I say?" she said. "Jack, he's just full of life, and he understands it, you know, how to live. I mean he's not perfect, trust me, he's not," she said, "but he understands imperfection. You know what I mean?"

I smiled as if I did know what she meant.

"He's a visionary," she said.


When we were done and everyone headed back to the barn, I lingered for a few moments by the field and then walked back by myself. Sweat was sticking me to my clothes, but it was still midmorning and a cool wetness hung in the air. The dank smell of wet leaves was everywhere. Nature. I wasn't used to it. I took my time walking back. When I finally arrived at the screened-in porch outside the kitchen, there was no one around. I helped myself to a glass of iced tea and sat on one of the picnic benches looking out over the bushes and the path down to the farm. I enjoyed the emptiness, the quiet. It felt right to be in that kitchen, which was half indoors and half outdoors. The boundaries between inside and outside were fluid. My body ached, but it felt good. I was dirty, but I didn't want to be clean. I drank some tea and breathed a little. I was conscious of my breath, conscious of my iced tea, conscious of my legs and arms, my shin was mostly healed, I was conscious of my eyes. I had been paying attention to my food since I met Sylvia, and it made me think more about my body, even as I lurched from hangover to hangover, and now, tired from my tiny foray into farming, I could see that purposefulness about eating, drinking, and being in the world could be easier here. Maybe it was a cliché, maybe it was just naiveté, but I felt it. I looked out the back and thought about Sylvia. My investigation wasn't going well. I'd clearly misstepped with Melanie, and anyone else I talked to, if they knew Sylvia, didn't have much to say. They spoke fondly of her, like you'd speak fondly of the dead. I didn't know what to think or how to approach the topic. I didn't really have any questions besides "Do you know what happened to Sylvia?" and it seemed like no one could answer that. I guess I did have other questions: "Are you selling drugs? Do you know anybody who does? Is Jarvis selling or dealing something sinister? Do you think Jarvis might have threatened Sylvia or hurt her?" But I couldn't ask that. Unsure what to think, I tried to focus on a far-off tree. I tried to look farther. Someday it's going to help, this staring into space, I thought, even if that help is nothing but a psychological balm, a sort of placebo effect on the problem of existence. And capitalism. And love. Then Melanie came into my view, a human blur between me and the far-off tree. I watched her walk up to a small vegetable garden and begin cutting something there. She couldn't see me. I breathed some more. I imagined Sylvia sitting where I sat, in this kitchen, enjoying the flow between indoors and out, breathing, eating slowly, conscious of her eating. I couldn't believe what Melanie had said about Sylvia and Jarvis, but I didn't really know Sylvia. She might have had a crush on him. All kinds of people have crushes on all kinds of other people. There's no way to explain it. Maybe I should go out and talk to Melanie, I thought. I drank some tea and breathed. Then I saw Jarvis coming up the path toward Melanie. She didn't see him. I thought he was going to walk past her or say something to her, but instead he came up close to her, almost sneaking up to her, and placed his hand on her back, massaging it gently. It didn't startle her. She just kept working. He hooked the other hand around her waist. He leaned in close to her. She was still cutting something or actually, I thought, pulling weeds. She didn't look up or pull away from his hand, but she didn't turn toward him or respond to him kindly either. She didn't pay him any mind. Maybe she enjoyed his hand on her back, and part of that enjoyment relied on ignoring him, continuing to do what she was doing while he fondled her from behind with his old hands. He put his mouth close to her neck. Maybe he was whispering something in her ear, or maybe he was just breathing warmly, heavily, onto her young and salty neck. There was something utterly disgusting about it. I was too far away to hear them or to see clearly, but I could almost feel it. He kept his right hand on her back and his left, I couldn't see his left, but I imagined that it groped the front of her somewhere. He moved even closer to her, eclipsing her body from view.

"Dude!" Nick startled me. I hadn't heard him come in. "Dude, I was looking for you," he said.

I turned. Nick was fiddling with a machine part of some kind. He put it down on the counter and started rifling through drawers. "I was wondering where you snuck off to," he said as if he were saying,

"I see what you're doing, secretly ogling Jarvis and Melanie; I see what you're up to." I glanced back at Jarvis, who was still massaging Melanie. Nick kept opening drawers manically and slamming them closed again. I held my iced tea in my hand, swirling it slowly like Mandeville swirled his Italian military liquors. I tried not to think of Jarvis fondling Melanie or Jarvis fondling Sylvia or some idea that I might be idly watching this fondling and not actively finding the reason that Sylvia had gone missing, or at least just enjoying my iced tea, being conscious of it, although that now seemed like a crime too. Nick looked at me, annoyed.

"I have so much shit to do before development," Nick said. He pulled some wire out of the bottom right drawer. "Can you help me with this rototiller? It's fucked."

Nick seemed annoyed the whole time we were welding and bolting the rototiller and some strange weeding apparatus. Or really *he* was welding and bolting them. I was just holding and fetching. I wasn't sure if he was annoyed with me or with something else. Still, I wanted to know more about the relationships on the farm and about Sylvia, so I slipped in a few vague questions as we oiled the rototiller.

"What's the deal with Melanie?" I asked.

"What do you mean?" he said.

"Are she and Jarvis, like, an item?" I said. I felt weird saying *an item*.

Nick didn't answer at first. I suppose that was his prerogative. He was using the Dremel to hollow something out. I waited for the noise to end. Nick looked up and nodded, or it wasn't really a nod but I took it as a "Yes, they are an item."

"Huh," I said. "Isn't he a little . . ." I gave Nick a look. ". . . old?" I said. I expected him to say something sarcastic or critical. It was the kind of thing he'd usually pounce on, a sexagenarian megalomaniac dating a young woman with pigtails. But he didn't take the bait. He still seemed annoyed. He just said, "They've been seeing each other for a while. They seem happy."

We worked quietly, tensely. "Make sure you're at the development by eleven," Nick said at last. It was the only thing he said before rushing off to his next task. "Don't be fucking late. Jarvis doesn't like it."

# Chapter 35

# A WORM ON A HOOK

I wasn't late. I didn't want to get on Jarvis's bad side. But I still felt late when I entered the dark theater. Most of the plush seats with pull-out desk-trays were already full. No one spoke.

The development turned out to be a strange multimedia presentation that seemed a little bit like a corporate trust-building retreat. It began with the song "Bird on the Wire" by Leonard Cohen blasting. The lyrics flashed on the large screen, karaoke-style. Afterward Jarvis stood in front of the screen and asked us questions about freedom. He quoted the song a lot. He was wearing one of those small wireless microphones that pop stars wear. They always irk me like eyebrow piercings irk me. The farmers raised their hands and discussed the song. Nothing that anyone said related to farming, and all of it seemed like nonsense.

Next: a clip from a black-and-white film. I recognized it right away as *The Defiant Ones* with Tony Curtis and Sidney Poitier, which I had watched just a few weeks earlier when I was checking the Tony Curtis story. At first I was shocked by the coincidence, but then I realized Jarvis must have read the Tony Curtis story, which had just run. Still, I had no idea why the hell he should be showing a bunch of young farmers a clip of two convicts trying to scale a wall in the pouring rain.

The convicts were chained to one another and kept dragging each other down the wall. Curtis's Southern accent was comically bad. It was a little embarrassing, although I wouldn't mention this to Tony Curtis if I talked to him again. I might mention watching the scene. Tony would like to hear that. "Wasn't that a great scene?" he'd say. "Everyone was blown away," I'd say.

They were blown away—or something like it, scribbling in their little notebooks. Notes about what? The convicts ascended the hill, finally, as Tony climbed on Poitier's shoulders. At the top, Poitier tended to Tony's injured hand. Heavy-handed, I thought. The whole film, with the wooden Tony Curtis doing a bad Southern accent, seemed absurd. Movies from the fifties about race were often simplistic at best. If we only get to know each other, we'll understand each other; we'll respect each other. We'll love each other. We're all in this together.

I knew that the screenwriter Nedrick Young couldn't have believed this. Young was blacklisted. Like Paul Robeson, he had taken a stand against the HUAC. He hadn't been able to find work for a decade. Finally he wrote under a pseudonym, Nathan Douglas, and was able to sell *The Defiant Ones*, an interracial convict movie. He won an Oscar for it and controversially revealed his true identity: Nedrick Young, blacklisted dissident. A few years later Young led an unsuccessful lawsuit against the motion picture industry claiming that the blacklist was a violation of antitrust laws. Young was a radical. He spoke truth to power. But his wife, Frances, who was also blacklisted, committed suicide.

"What is freedom?" Jarvis asked dramatically through his tiny microphone. "The title of today's development is 'Cultivating Freedom.'

Take a moment," he said. "Meditate. Take notes. Do what you need to do, but think. What does cultivating freedom mean to you? What makes you free?"

Everyone rustled. The lights came up slowly. I took up the pencil Melanie had given me and turned the paper over. I wrote, *Nefarious Business, terrible things going on in every business. Terrible things? Take care of something? You were right?????* I drew a lot of question marks. I drew a face with a scar. It looked nothing like Sylvia. Nothing like anyone. People are elusive, I thought. I looked around. Everyone looked very serious or very tired or both. Time moved slowly.

"Now," said Jarvis, "I'd like you to get together with two or three others sitting near you and discuss. What do each of you think of freedom? Where do you agree? Where do you conflict? Then we'll talk as a group."

I was sitting next to an orange-tinted woman I didn't know and Dawn, one of the pickers I'd met in the potato fields. Earlier Dawn had said, "Oh, you're the one checking up on us, right?" She said it in a friendly way and followed it with a familiar "That's so cool," but I had felt like a health inspector on a surprise visit. Now I felt even more conspicuous, perhaps because I resented Jarvis. I smiled at Dawn. The orange-tinted woman began a long story about her aggressive, poorly behaved cat. It made her feel bad, this cat, even though she loved it. The cat would beat up the other cat in the household, which was only living there temporarily. The orange woman's cat threw the other cat off the roof.

Finally, Jarvis asked us to share. The orange woman spoke up first. "Well, in our group," she said, "this gentleman, the fact-checker, talked about how he broke up with his girlfriend and didn't feel free." She looked at me. "Is it OK if I tell this?" she asked me.

I must have nodded.

She continued, "When this woman broke up with him, he felt more constrained. Like, conventionally a relationship makes you dependent, but maybe they provide a certain kind of freedom, because you are secure in, like, your understanding of the world; you know what's what. But then when you find that someone was lying to you, it's, like, sort of crippling. So I guess we wondered," the orange woman said, "if freedom isn't, like, only a personal thing, but it's, like, a social thing."

Jarvis smiled and moved to the next speaker.

At the end of a long line of confessions, Jarvis finally turned the conversation back to farming. He did so by way of a Goethe quote that was printed on a sheet and handed around: "We must understand that all fact is really theory. The blue of the sky reveals to us the basic law of color. Search nothing beyond the phenomena, they themselves are the theory."

"Goethe reminded us," Jarvis said, "that when we are trying to repair the whole ecosystem, to give life to the soil, we can't just do so through theories, but we must look at individuals, individual people, plants, and species, he said. Each individual has its own desires and impulses. Responding to each is responding to the whole. Responding to our ourselves too is responding to the whole."

Jarvis ended his seminar with an injunction: "Remember, when you are cultivating the earth, you must also cultivate freedom. Freedom alone. Together."

\* \* \*

Lunch was good at least. But I kept having to talk about the "development." Sonya, a young woman with rings in her nose and her eyebrow, kept saying, "This development was so moving, wasn't it? It really rejuvenated me." Then she asked me, "Is this your first development?" This was the third or fourth time I had been asked that in a similar way. I did not like this use of the word *development*, and I didn't want to answer yes. Everyone was saying it with this wide-eyed excitement, as if they were eager for me to experience this development thing with them and, in so doing, to reaffirm their own sense of development and its importance and perhaps their more developed state. I noticed in some of the older farmers (not that any of them were very old) there was also a sense of experience, almost weariness. They'd already been developed. I tried not to give away either my curiosity or my suspicion. "Yes," I told Sonya, "I've never seen anything quite like it." Then I smiled mildly, tightening my lips and turning my head away as if to say, "There's nothing more to say." There *was* more to say, of course. I wanted to ask about Sylvia and about Oxy or any other nefarious business, besides pot smoking and old men fondling young farm girls. But my bad conversation with Melanie and Nick's foul mood just after that conversation had thrown me. Now I didn't know how much to reveal when I asked questions. How much could I "lead the witness," as they say, or might I find other means to know things?

A bearded guy named Matt, the one I'd seen on the tractor, came up to me and asked about the magazine. "It must be amazing working there," he said. "It must be so cool."

I nodded. "Yeah, it's cool," I said. "You get to work on a lot of different kinds of things." I gave him my usual. "You get to be a mini-expert on something new every week. One day it's explosive devices.

The next it's tomatoes. I like that. I like getting deep into a subject and then getting deep into another."

"Cool," he said. "Do you know Hazlin?"

I nodded and turned back to my salad: a beautiful variety of pole beans, potatoes, cherry tomatoes, lettuces, olives, onions. I tried different combinations. I enjoyed it. Alone.

My solitude was disturbed a few minutes later by Jarvis himself. He wanted me to help edit the farm's website that afternoon. He said, "We'd be so grateful," but he didn't sound like he'd be grateful.

"I'm Simone," the woman standing next to him said. Simone? Like Simone de Beauvoir? "I run the website," she said. She had a surprisingly deep voice. "Jack told me about your job. So cool."

# Chapter 36

# BOMB-DEFUSING ROBOTS

I found Simone in the "office," which was a tiny alcove behind the staircase. It had a computer desk with room for exactly one person to work. Simone had set a stool beside her desk chair, but I had to squeeze around her to sit. Plus, the stool was high, so I was looking down on her and her work while pressed up against her chair and the desk. I felt like an overbearing lifeguard.

Simone's post, which she had printed out for me, was a pleasant, fairly generic argument for the importance of organic agriculture and for growing things in general. It seemed aimed at young, idealistic, but uninformed readers, but it didn't seem like something that a kid who didn't care might read and then decide to care. It was hard to make people care, and maybe not always that useful.

I corrected a few typos and grammatically awkward sentences and noted where she might bring together two harvesting descriptions rather than separating them by a digression on the rhythms of the day. Just a few organizational notes.

"I think this is great," I said. I wasn't sure I actually thought it was great, but I didn't think it was bad and it was rude to say, "This isn't bad." Nonetheless, I felt like I was overdoing the "This is great," in my tone, and so even though I was about to say, "I think this is great, but—" and suggest a few larger changes, I didn't. I stopped. She looked me in the eye and opened her mouth slightly.

"Thanks," she said.

I looked up at the red built-in bookshelves that surrounded the desk. Everything seemed to fit perfectly in its little nook: the books, the storage baskets, the printer. It was so neat and clean, so unlike my desk, which was piled high with stacks of papers and books, the endless ocean of facts that together amounted to little but clutter. Here there was a thing for each purpose, like you would have if you lived on a boat, or lived a simple life. It seemed fake.

"Why are you here?" I asked.

"Hmmm . . . Why *am* I here?" she said, and she burst out laughing. "I don't fucking know." I laughed too. We sat for a minute, laughing together.

"I mean, at New Egypt," I said. "You were on a farm up north last year?"

"Yeah, I was in Maine," she said, and then exhaled a deeply held breath. "Maine was nice, but I heard about this place and the whole geodynamic thing, and I was interested. This is a much bigger operation too. I heard they needed somebody who could do computer stuff, and I guess"—she thought for a minute—"I guess I needed to get out of Maine."

"You did computer stuff up there?"

"Not really, but I was a computer science major," she said. "I'm a big nerd."

I wasn't sure what to say next. The development had made me paranoid. Like I was in the body snatchers zone. I could start by asking what it meant to be developed: Developed into what? Might we use drugs to develop our senses? To see farther?

"How did you get into farming, then?" I asked Simone.

"I guess I just wanted something new."

"Something new?" I raised my eyebrows and shifted myself on the stool. I couldn't get comfortable. My leg was falling asleep. "There are a lot of other new things you could have done. Why this?"

"I guess I wanted something more . . ." she said. ". . . more elemental."

I must have made another face because she laughed and swiveled her chair toward me, pinning my legs back in the process.

"You really want to know?" she said. She seemed excited but unsure. "There was this day in college that sticks in my mind as like a turning point. I was having a problem with my computer. I had been up all night working on this project, and I was really stressed about it, you know?" She laughed. She seemed nervous. Or maybe it was just me.

"It's funny now," she continued, "to think back on the kind of intense, I don't know, like, tunnel vision you get when you're working on a coding problem. It can be the simplest thing that gets you, and you go deeper and deeper. It's like a drug, really. I kind of miss it sometimes.

"I remember," she continued, "I was trying to write this script for this bomb-defusing robot. I mean, it wasn't real. It wasn't really even a robot. It was this hypothetical that everyone had to do in this intro class. In Python. Like, just a set of complex responses to different inputs. Nothing major. So, like, my robot was good, it was, like, totally fine ninety-eight percent of the time, but then every once in a while, if you asked it to do the same thing, like, eighteen times in a row, it just wouldn't do it. It would freeze. It would just return a blank line. Nothing. So I'm racking my brain all night—you really pull a lot of all-nighters when you're doing CS—and I'm just poring through every line of code, looking for the wrong parentheses or some little thing I must be missing. Hours of my life were like this. Just gone. But this wasn't my problem. I knew I'd figure it out eventually. I was used to these annoying little problems. But then, in the middle of this whole thing, before I figured out what was wrong with my programming, my computer died. It just failed and I couldn't reboot it. It sucked. It was like this double whammy: The robot thing was refusing my instructions and now the computer was, like, joining up with it and going, 'We're done.'"

I shifted on my stool again. My foot was already dead. Pins and needles.

"So anyway my friend Jason came over—he was a tech genius, and he spent a shitload of time on my machine, trying to get it working again—and he just kept saying, 'The computer doesn't recognize itself,' and I was, like, What the hell? I mean, it sounds silly to tell this story, but that night I kind of gave up on CS. I remember Jason kept saying it, all glassy-eyed. You ever watch somebody playing video games? It's creepy. That's what programmers are like all the time. He's like that and he keeps saying, 'It won't recognize itself.' I started to feel bad for the computer, you know. We were all going through these tough times. Jason and I actually made a big joke of it, like the computer really needed a gap year so it could go find itself. But I don't know. I was done."

Simone turned back to the screen and started pressing the keys.

"I wasn't freaked out by technology. Like AI is coming to get us, or like we're becoming cyborgs or any of that," she said. "Although I guess I do think we're cyborgs, and it's pretty weird. But it was more like I got caught up in the idea of recognizing the self. Like it was this joke, but it was real. For me, I mean. We had this development, here at New Egypt, that was all about identifying the self in the natural world. What does it mean to really see oneself as a living thing, you know? When I was programming, I could get so stressed about, like, these parentheses, and I was suddenly, like, Why?" She paused. "So I guess I wanted something different, you know? And I grew up near farms with horses and stuff, so . . . here I am, trying to recognize myself or something like that."

I smiled and tried to bang my foot against the floor to wake it up. Deadweight.

"Sorry I'm babbling," she said.

"No," I said. "That's what you should blog about: bomb-defusing robots."

She swiveled back toward me and looked as if she were about to add something important. But she stopped.

"Were you friends with Sylvia at all?" I asked.

"Yeah," she said, somewhat surprised. "I was. I mean, I am."

"You don't know where she went?"

"No," she said. "She just disappeared. I'm kind of pissed at her. Or worried. Or both."

"Me too," I said. "Worried, I mean." I took a breath, not quite sure how to proceed. We made eye contact. "She told me something," I said. "This was a few weeks ago. She said there were strange things going on here," I said. "She sounded kind of, I don't know—"

"The Jersey Devil," Simone said.

"The what?"

"Sorry," she said. "That just popped into my head. I mean, I'm sure that wasn't what Sylv was talking about." Simone smiled again like she was remembering a joke. "Never mind."

"The Jersey Devil?"

"You know, the thing that haunts the Pine Barrens?" Simone laughed. "There was this girl here, Janis," she said. "This was a while ago—last summer, actually. Janis was kind of a kook. She was weird. Genuinely weird. You know what I mean? So one day she starts complaining about 'visitations' in her room." Simone put air quotes around the word *visitations*. "Like some kind of ghost or spirit was coming to her at night. Everyone thought it was funny. Like, what a freak. But Janis was very serious about it. We all joked and called it the Jersey Devil. Janis was sleeping with the Jersey Devil, people said. It was kind of mean. Then Sylvia started calling Jarvis the Jersey Devil. Behind his back, I mean. He was probably the one sneaking into her room, the old perv. Or that's what Sylvia said.

"It's funny," Simone continued in her deep, incongruous voice. "Janis kind of disappeared too, like Sylvia. I remember Sylvia saying that it was probably Melanie who drove her out. Getting rid of the competition, Sylvia would say."

I tried to look inquisitive without seeming shocked or judgmental. Simone just smiled.

"Does Jarvis—"

I stopped, unsure of my words. I considered saying "play the field," but that seemed offensive or paternalistic. Immediately the term *plow the field* also popped into my head, which didn't help me collect my thoughts.

"—date a lot of the farmers?" I said.

"Well, I don't know about 'dating.'" Simone used air quotes again. "He's very sexually open, I will say that. I mean, I don't know about what he does in private, but in public, in development and, like, at dinner, he likes to talk about desire and eros, and how sexual farming is, making love to Mother Earth, that kind of thing. He's always showing movies with naked young women in them too. That's his favorite genre. Naked teenage girl films. He's not exactly PC," Simone said. "He's kind of a dirty old man."

"Do you think that bothered Sylvia?" I said.

"Oh, I don't know," Simone said. "Sylvia made fun of him. I mean, he's like a father figure around here, and, like, he comes from a different time and place, so—" Simone stopped.

"Look, I don't want to gossip," she said. "Sylvia wasn't a gossip. But she had high standards, mostly for herself. She just did her own thing. I admired her. I mean, I do. I admire Sylv. I just wish she was still around."

"So you don't know if anything weird was going on with Sylvia and Jarvis?" I asked. "He wasn't hitting on her?"

Simone made a face. "I doubt it." she said. She took a deep breath.

"Maybe it was about tomatoes," she said. "If Sylvia was going to get really pissed about something, enough to pick a fight or take off, it would probably have to do with tomatoes. And Jack's tomatoes, she didn't say anything exactly, but I could sense she disapproved."

"Of the Ramapos?"

"Yeah, the ones he grows in Pittstown. I've never been there," she said, "but nobody has. It's kind of weird. They're, like, our cash crop, our golden eggs, but we don't grow them. We barely touch them. They just come in on a truck every week, ready to sell."

Simone turned back to her computer and started to type. I shifted toward it as well, but then I felt self-conscious about looking at her from above, like I was intruding on her digital space. I looked up at the bookshelf in front of me.

"Do you know anything about any drugs here on the farm?"

"Drugs?" She raised her eyebrows. "Talk to Nick," she said. "Aren't you guys friends? Nick's got acres of weed."

"No, I meant something stronger." I shifted again "Like painkillers?"

"Are you in pain?" she said sympathetically. "You have to talk to Asia. She's studying Chinese medicine and she has lots of herbs, and she does acupuncture and massage." I must have made a face. "I used to be skeptical about that stuff too," Simone said. "But now I swear by it. I used to have carpal tunnel"—she stretched out her arm toward me and did a series of strange gestures—"but not anymore."

# Chapter 37

# MOONSHINE

I saw Simone again later that afternoon. She came out with Nick and Travis and me to pick a few final tomatoes and squash for the dinner. It was the first time I actually made it into Sylvia's tomato houses. I was surprised that there were still so many things ripening there without her, so late in the season: yellow pear-shaped tomatoes, flat green pancakes, red-black tumorous bulbs, pale pink cherries. All sizes. But the plants themselves drew my attention as much as the tomatoes. Sharp and fingery, pale and dense, upward and everywhere. It was the organized wild. I was picking huge ripe Brandywines right next to Simone. She smiled at me. I looked at her sunburnt face and then beyond her. I looked out the open end of the hoop house and had a sort of revelation, even if it was an obvious one, and not so life-changing. I didn't recognize myself, to use Simone's terms, but I did know, or feel strongly: There was something beautiful about the farm. I don't mean the landscape was nice to look at or dramatic or that it put me in touch with the sublime. I suppose I did like all the green plants, not just the tomato plants; they evoked some sense memory or primal feeling of summer, especially now at dusk. But that's not what I mean, exactly. Nor do I think the rural life, the simple life, is somehow more real or more significant or more satisfying than the urban life. Thoreau, after all, was a jerk, and our whole idea of nature is evolved out of smokestacks and middle-class aspirations. I wasn't convinced by communal living either. I mean, I liked it in theory. Of course we should try to live together better; we should all be worshiping the Deity. We should be living "intentionally." Part of me was always trying to live together better with everyone, with my friends and colleagues and fellow humans, with Magda, with the world. But not in an organized way and not with Jarvis. He seemed monstrous, a megalomaniacal sexual predator. Plus, the farm didn't seem very free or very equal. Communitarians, as Sylvia had noted, are often some of the most inflexible people. Still, standing there among the microgreens, some of them poorly formed and others ripening, among mixed blues and greens and ribs and canopies, among ales and chards and unknown hearty things, I thought: Food is beautiful, this food particularly, food grown organically and thoughtfully, not driven by maximum yield and profit margin. I knew how bad factory farming was for people and animals and the places we inhabit. I knew there was something good in this chard, something factually good. I looked at Simone and Nick. They were happy with what they'd grown. They felt satisfied, I thought, although I couldn't tell this for sure. I don't know what struggles and doubts they had, or how much money they made or didn't make. I couldn't tell how much they might really hate Jarvis, how they might resent his arrogance and whether, like Sylvia, they were torn and wanted to leave. I was sure that's what happened to her. She couldn't deal with development and all it entailed. She couldn't take the weird corporate New Age, and I guess she couldn't deal with me, or didn't want to. No, I didn't really know what Simone and Nick were thinking. I couldn't.

We pulled the rest of the Brandywines and Mortgage Lifters and put them in the wheelbarrow. I rolled it back to the kitchen.


Despite the fact that I'd picked both potatoes and eggplant, I didn't enjoy either that much at dinner. They'd been roasted in an open fire and, it seemed, undersalted. They were crispy, dry, and tasteless. Maybe it was me. I couldn't taste the chicken either. All I really wanted were more tomatoes. I'd been eating these same tomatoes just about every day since I met Sylvia, but I wasn't tired of them. And here I had access to every shape and size of tomato. They were thickly sliced and lined up in big long rows on butcher block, a sea of yellow, orange, and green-black flesh, glistening with oil and sea salt and little flecks of basil. Heaven. My body craved the tomatoes above all else, like they were providing some mineral I had lost. I went back for seconds.

We were sitting on picnic blankets around a huge bonfire, which was sending big smoke signals into the summer sky and across the Pine Barrens. I had Per and Nick and this big guy, Hugo, sitting by me. Simone was beyond Hugo, just beyond my conversation zone. Hugo told me about playing the trumpet in various professional orchestras. He was often a substitute on Broadway, a role that came with a range of pleasures—it was exciting to step into a fully formed orchestra with a specific story to tell—and drawbacks—people didn't always appreciate your presence, and you didn't get paid much. It sounded a lot like being an adjunct professor, as many of my old friends were. Now Hugo was farming, "for a while anyway." It wasn't lucrative either, but he liked it.

He went off to get a guitar and join the two guys who were sitting on stumps, playing hippie classics. They'd already done "Heart of Gold" and "Wish You Were Here" and now were moving onto "Have You Ever Seen the Rain?" Hugo's departure opened up a space between me and Simone, but she was in the middle of a conversation with Dawn, so I stayed put. I looked at the fire for a while, doing its inscrutable fire thing. The musicians started up "Three Little Birds" and some people joined in. I was alone. I'd been alone for a long time, but now, with the smell of the fire and the unending sky and the hippie chorus, I felt acutely alone, deeply, bodily. It wasn't necessarily a bad feeling. But it wasn't *not* a bad feeling.

Someone passed me a bottle of moonshine, and I held on to it for a while even though it burned. "Don't Think Twice, It's All Right" was next. I looked over toward a gaggle of women in flowery clothes over by the guitarists. One of them was in a full-on Stevie Nicks outfit. Hippie fashion persisted. Patchouli and tapestries still filled college dorm rooms across the country. I'd always found this distasteful but now, hitting the moonshine again and looking out at these women, I could see the appeal. For so many people, at least in a certain socioeconomic group, this was the uniform of revolution, political revolution and personal revolution wrapped in one, even if that revolution had only led to Bill Clinton, deregulating industry, and destroying welfare. Blowsy, flowery shirts still signaled some alternative to capitalism, some promise of value outside of the marketplace, some promise of freedom, some hope.

Sylvia held some promise for me, I thought. That's why I was here, alone. But what did she promise? It wasn't sex or love or companionship. Well, it was these things. I wanted these things. But it was something more too. Maybe it was just her vocation. Organic farming was better, morally, than fact-checking, wasn't it? Better to grow good things well, to nurture them, to nurture others, even for a price, than to police ideas, to nitpick, to dissemble, even in the name of truth. But I didn't want to be a farmer. I wanted something else that I couldn't grasp, something more political, and yet something more elemental, to use Simone's phrase, something good. I couldn't find it. All around there was trouble, black markets, nefarious business. Everything seemed to conspire against us, everything seemed coordinated to keep a singular, beautiful person from thriving, and to keep me from thriving with her. I took another swig of moonshine and tried to stand up. It was hard. I was drunk.

# Chapter 38

# PINGLIANG CITY

I was urinating by the edge of the woods when I found Jarvis's trailer. Maybe I was looking for it. I don't know. I was drunk and stoned. The trailer was dark. I tried the door. Locked. The kitchen window was ajar, though.

Jarvis had done something to Sylvia, and I needed to know what he had done. I could probably break in. I could maybe use a long, thin rake I'd seen in front of Travis's cabin, but that might not be enough. If I could find a branch with a slight hook, I could jimmy the top latch upward and rake the bottom of the handle toward the window and pop it. I'd be inside Jarvis's man cave and I'd discover his secrets. I stumbled back up the hill, stopping halfway up to listen to the crickets again. It was amazing, that senseless chorus. A cloud moved across the moon. I felt again like I was in an El Greco painting, a surreal place where people could float away at any time into the ether. Perhaps Sylvia had just floated away. Dissolved into the crickets. I continued up the hill, got the rake, and returned to the big tree—I didn't know what kind of tree. I looked for the right kind of branch. This wasn't going to work.

I went back up to the cabin where I was supposed to sleep. No one was there. I looked through the closets. I found two wire hangers.

One of them held a plaid shirt, so I slung that on top of another plaid shirt. There was a pack of American Spirits on the porch. The light-blue kind. I took one and lit it, inhaling deeply, filling my lungs with garbage that was packaged as if it were organic and healthy and spiritual and good. Maybe it was. I took another drag. I walked back to the trailer. In seconds I was inside.

I was afraid to turn on the light at first but then I was pretty drunk so I just did it. There was a small bed on one side of the room with a storage area under it. I reached under and pulled out a box, an old tomato box with pictures of tomatoes and some words in what looked like Chinese. Inside the box were a bunch of sex toys. I shoved it back under the bed. Then I rifled through the drawers of an old rolltop desk. I found lots of invoices and receipts. Nothing interesting. I checked out the file cabinet in the corner. Nothing interesting. But in the bottom drawer there was a file folder labeled PITTSTOWN. It had a few documents in Chinese. Again Chinese. I couldn't read anything on them besides a place name, Pingliang City, Gansu Province, and two words in English: Ramapo tomatoes. It showed up several times. The papers looked like invoices—invoices for Chinese tomatoes. I folded them up and put them in my pocket.

Just then I heard a noise behind me. I turned. Something hit me. Hard.


Or I think that's what happened. But it's hard now to recall the sensation—we always block out past pain—never mind to know what struck me, or who struck me, or why. Plus, I was wasted. Maybe I'm misremembering the whole thing.

I passed out. That I know.

# Chapter 39

# CAP AND TRADE

I don't think I have ever felt as miserable as I did when I woke. I was in such a dark cloud. The pain was throbbing in and out, both severe and indistinct. A deep nausea pulsed in and around my entire body, pinning me to the strange couch and churning everything. Remembering this now, though, the whole thing seems like a dream. The pain in my head, the matted blood behind my ear, the poison in my system, seem like a vague fiction, not the truth. But there I was, lying on a brown leather sofa in an office, picking off dried blood. I was no longer in the Airstream, where I'd seen the Chinese tomato invoices and boxes. A bluish light shone through the window above the door, an interior window. It might have been dawn light. Or the lights of hell.

I tried to push my body up but it didn't work. So I rolled my legs toward the floor instead. I eventually managed to lift my head above my shoulders. Bad idea. I settled back down and closed my eyes. I tried to reset my brain, to return to some emptiness like a Buddhist. Zen noodles. No past. No present. No body. Remove everything that is revolting against you. I tried to empty myself of Sylvia. She was in there too. She was a free spirit, Mandeville said. Maybe she was a ghost, a visitation like the Jersey Devil, like potatoes, or a free radical, charged, floating from cell to cell. Sylvia was looking for good in the world. She wanted to do good without somehow overstepping her bounds and infringing on others. She was positive and open, not suspicious. But she'd found Chinese tomatoes and had fled, or worse. I suppose I wanted some part of that, the free spirit, the desire to do good without infringing on others, the openness. But she'd run up against something in every one of her cults, some evil, some aggressive men, some hidden agenda, Chinese tomatoes. That's what Jarvis was selling, the lecherous hypocrite. He must have caught me snooping. I felt the back of my neck. A prick of pain and fear ran through me. I better get up. I tried again and forced up my head. Dizzy. I steadied myself. I needed water.

The door opened. Jarvis entered.

"Quite a night last night," he said. "How are you feeling?" He loomed above me, starched polo tucked into starched chinos.

"Like shit," I think I said.

"Little too much farm juice?" he said. The way he looked at me—with some combination of bemusement and anger, or maybe it wasn't anger but just a general cockiness, a man always ready for a fight—made me feel sicker than I already did. I wanted to confront him, or at least to tell him to fuck off, but I couldn't raise my head.

"We found you passed out over by the trailers," he said. I felt the back of my neck.

"Found me? Seriously?" I said. "Somebody hit me on the back of the head."

"Hit you?" he said. "Now, why would anyone do that?" He added a bit of Southern twang to his voice, I realized, when he was condescending.

I looked up, my head throbbing.

"I don't know. Maybe I should ask you that."

Jarvis smiled widely and unfolded his large, wrinkled hands.

"Young man," he said. "New Egypt is a welcoming place, a peaceful place. We have people here from all walks of life, who come here to be part of this great project, this rebirth, and we all must"—he stepped closer to me—"trust each other." He looked at me more sternly. "Now, I don't mind a bit of drink," he said. "Sometimes we all need a release." He came closer, standing over me. "Sometimes we need to feel a bit of the chaos of the universe inside of us," he said, "and to know something, even by a journey of not-knowing, about our place in that chaos. I get that. I feel that. So I don't judge you for that. But this is a peaceful place, a trusting place, and right now you're fucking with my mojo. Seriously. You are a fucking fly in the ointment, young man, and I can't have that." I felt the edge in his voice. He was standing above me, his hands trembling from anger or old age. I was afraid. "Right now you're like a disease in this ecosystem, sir. And I can't have that. Get your things together." He put his hand on my shoulder and pressed me deep into the sofa.

"Where do your Ramapos come from?" I said. "I mean really?"

He didn't answer.

"China?" I said. "You don't grow them, do you? You're whole organic, local project is bullshit, isn't it?"

He squeezed my shoulder harder and the pressure wasn't exactly pain. I was already fully engulfed in pain. There was something comforting about being pressed. I was, I realize, a little delirious.

"You don't know shit, kid," he said. "I want you off my property." He released my shoulder, turned, and walked away.

"Oh, now it's *your* fucking property," I spit.

He turned back again and smiled. It was a serene smile, as if none of this mattered in the world. His anger was gone. He didn't say anything. He just smiled. I sank into the couch. I couldn't do a thing.

I'd had a couple of glasses of water, a handful of Advil, and a cup of coffee. None of it helped. I knew from a story I'd checked once that a hangover was at its worst at the point when the last of the alcohol leaves the system. I knew I probably hadn't hit that point yet, so things were only going downhill. I was probably still drunk. I knew too that the pain in the back of my head was more than a hangover. There was a lump there, I thought. Brain damage. There wasn't enough Advil in the world to fix me. I wondered how those macho types who like to get into bar fights dealt with the cocktail of pains the next day. I was angry and bleary. I checked my pockets for the papers. They were gone. Had I dreamed it?

I didn't know how to react to Nick. He was urging me to get ready. He was leaving in fifteen minutes. I wanted to leave too. I wanted to get as far from Jarvis as I could. I liked Nick. He would help me, I thought.

"Hurry up, dude," he said again. I was sitting, upright at least, on the couch in his cabin. "We gotta go. Now."

Ultimately he was Jarvis's man.

"So that's how it is?" I asked. "Jarvis tells you to jump, and you fucking jump. Now you're kicking me out."

"Fuck you, dude," he said. "You want to hang around? Fine."

"Fine," I said. I sat. I tried more water. "Give me twenty minutes."

I pulled myself up, washed my face, brushed my teeth, had some more coffee—bad idea—brushed my teeth again, and grabbed my bag. I wanted to find Simone before I left, to tell her about the Chinese tomatoes. She wasn't around. Everywhere I checked, it seemed like people were watching me. Sonya was idly rolling up a hose by the back barn and eyeing me; bearded Matt followed me slowly toward the main house. Melanie was in the kitchen. We had a weird exchange, or lack of exchange. We didn't say a word to each other. I drank some water and she ate oatmeal. I spotted Hugo out on the path, right by the garden where I'd seen Jarvis fondling Melanie. Now Melanie was on the porch watching me, or so I imagined. I asked Hugo if he'd seen Simone. He hadn't. She was probably off doing chores, he said. Did I check with Melanie? She might know. I tried to smile. I didn't tell him about the Chinese tomatoes or the lump on the back of my head. I didn't tell anyone.

Except for Nick. But by then we were on our way back to the city.

"Chinese tomatoes?" he said. "You're shitting me."

I didn't say anything. I wasn't feeling any better and the rattling truck wasn't helping. Nick's comic outrage, which I usually found endearing, now seemed sinister.

"You've got this crazy obsession with Sylvia," he said. I rubbed the back of my neck and sipped from my water bottle.

"Look," Nick said finally. We were passing again into the industrial wasteland of the Passaic river valley. "I'm not saying Jack is perfect, but Chinese tomatoes? You're fucking with me."

"I saw the invoices," I said. "What else is he buying from Gansu Province?"

The smell took us again. Nick turned up the radio, as if ZZ Top could drown out the sulfuric stench. A few other bad songs followed.

Some Bad Company, I think, followed by a long period of FM scan. It pounded on my dull brain.

"You know the theory of cap and trade?" Nick said. "Like, for carbon emissions?"

I remained silent.

"You know how cap and trade can create a market for carbon allowances but also create incentives for innovation to decrease dependence on carbon? It helps fund the little guys working on being carbon-free."

"In theory," I said.

"Well, suppose you're ninety-eight percent organic and local but in order to fund that you need, like, two percent conventional."

We passed the industrial wasteland that had smelled so bad on our way out. It smelled fine.

"All the costs of that two percent would ultimately be more than covered in the, like, grand scheme of things, you know. You're still operating under the cap, and by doing all the other stuff, the good stuff, you help the world bring down that cap. You're making natural agriculture desirable again, creating a market for it, but maybe you can't do that from scratch."

"You knew about the tomatoes?" I said.

Nick didn't respond.

"You fucking knew," I said again. My head pounding.

"Fuck you," he said. "There aren't any Chinese fucking tomatoes." An ad was playing for the Major World car dealership, loud and toneless.

"Maybe there's something weird going on up in Pittstown," he said finally. "But it's not fucking Chinese tomatoes." We pulled toward the Holland Tunnel, merging into a slow river of cars.

We passed through the tunnel to the sound of static. It felt good to emerge on the city side, home turf.

"Cap and trade is bullshit," I said as I got out on Canal Street, "and Jarvis is an asshole."

Nick shrugged. "Maybe," he said.

# Chapter 40

# EDIBLE BABIES

Nick wasn't the only one who shrugged off the Chinese tomatoes. Dixon, the editor of the piece, barely lifted his head when I told him about my suspicions, and I didn't have much more luck with Mandeville.

"You know about Jarvis's secret tomato field, right?" I asked him.

"Yeah," he said, slightly annoyed. "It was in the piece."

"Right," I said. "I know. But are you sure it's in Pittstown?" I asked.

"Didn't you check it?" he said. "Is there some problem?"

"No," I said. "I mean—yes, I did check it. With Jarvis. But I think he was lying."

Mandeville didn't say anything for a minute. I had that strange sensation again of breathing into a dead phone line. Was anyone out there?

"You don't think it's in Pittstown?" he said. "Why lie about that?"

"I don't know," I said. "Why do *you* think he would?"

"Now that you mention it, he was pretty weird about the Ramapo fields. I kept trying to get up there but he kept putting me off. But Jarvis is a pretty weird guy," Mandeville said. "He's a bit of a nutter, you know? Paranoid. He was always sending me weird emails about

236

stuff I should watch out for. I just ignored them." Mandeville paused. "Weird mood swings too. Sometimes he'd get angry, suddenly angry. I thought maybe he was off his meds or something. And then sometimes he acted like he was doing me a big favor." I didn't say anything. "But this always happens with profiles, in some form or other," Mandeville said. "It's a strange thing to be profiled. I mean, it must be." He had moved from his macho voice to his sensitive voice.

"Are you sure he grows the Ramapos?" I asked.

"Of course," he said. "Jarvis loves them. *Loves* them. They're like his babies. In fact," Mandeville said, "he was kind of an asshole whenever he talked about his real kids. I think these were actually like his babies."

"We don't eat our babies," I said.

Mandeville laughed.

"I think they're grown in China," I said. "Jarvis imports them."

"China? What gives you that idea?"

I told him about my trip to the farm, omitting the drunkenness.

"You broke into his office?" Mandeville said. "You little son of a bitch."

That was about the end of Mandeville's reaction: a bit of surprise, a laugh. I don't know what I expected from him. Outrage? There were so many things to be outraged about. The possible minor fraud of a narcissistic tomato farmer may not have topped the list. Nor did the whereabouts of a young hippie, a "free spirit," no matter how "interesting" she might be. At least Mandeville believed me.

"Can we run some kind of correction or follow up?" I asked.

"Are you joking?" Mandeville said. "From what you just told me? The story's already out there. It's a food piece. It is what it is."

I listened to him breathing.

237

"OK," he said. "If it'll make you feel better, I'll do some poking around. Maybe this thing is bigger than Jarvis. Maybe it's worth a big exposé. I'll see what I can find out."

But I knew he wouldn't find anything. He never did.


I decided to talk directly to Asprilla, the editor in chief, next.

"It's about the Mandeville piece?" he asked. "The one we already shipped?"

"Yes, well . . ." I said. There was something about his office. It seemed brighter than any of the other offices, yet less airy, like you were at the top of a high mountain, suffocating.

"Something's come up," I said. "Some new information."

"It's come up?" he said.

"Yes, well, I, well, I went out to the farm, the tomato farm in the piece, and I think some of the tomatoes, the Ramapos, aren't grown in New Jersey."

Asprilla squinted, puzzling me out.

"They're imported from China," I said.

"What?" he said loudly standing up. "China?" He walked around the desk. "Are you trying to tell me that the central crop for this farm we just profiled isn't even grown there?"

I nodded. Asprilla stepped toward me.

"Jesus Christ," he said. "How long have you known this?"

"Just a few days."

"And how long have you had this piece?"

"Well . . ." I started calculating in my head. ". . . five, maybe six weeks," I said.

"Pathetic," he said. "You better hope nobody uncovers this and skewers us. Pathetic. Six weeks you were scratching your ass?" Now he was heading right at me headfirst. "You've been sitting on this piece for that long without figuring out that major problem. What do we pay you for?" He was close to me now. I thought he might just knock me over, but he didn't touch me. He stormed by and out his door, leaving me alone in the airless office.

# Chapter 41

# SWIFT BOAT

Soon after I was fired. Charles told me that it just wasn't working out.

"Was it 'Mandeville/Green'?" I asked.

"Where have you been lately?" Charles said. "Every time I come by your desk, you aren't there."

"I've been checking," I said.

He repeated, "It's not working out."

"But what about the Swift boat piece?" I asked.

"Fatima will handle it," he said.

I was shocked at first but also in some way relieved. I didn't want to be fired, but Charles was right. It wasn't working out. I wasn't cut out for the job. I couldn't let things go. I couldn't draw boundaries.

I've had a lot of different jobs since then. None were fact-checking jobs. I avoided those, and yet I've never shaken that fact-checker's feeling, the feeling I had when I interviewed the CIA widow and then read the Greenmarket piece for the first time, the feeling of fear and uncertainty about what I knew and what I didn't know, what I did and didn't do. What I should do. Maybe I was missing something, something important, something nefarious. I needed to keep researching, questioning, doubting, doubting myself as I doubt others.

For a while I managed the office for a group of eccentric Lebanese dentists. I really liked them, or at least one of them. He had grown up in Beirut during the Lebanese Civil War and had great style. He always wore pointy snakeskin boots and a dental coat that looked like Gaultier. Instead of playing soft rock, he would play free jazz while he drilled the patients. I was never comfortable with dentistry, though, not only because of the history of dental services, a history of cruelty and barbarity, but also because of questionable charges for things like "sealing" or "veneers." One of our dentists was billing a patient named Thomas McCovey, whose address did not seem to match anyone by that name. Was there really a Thomas McCovey and had he really received these treatments, or was it insurance fraud? I'll never know. I didn't work there long enough. I didn't last as a researcher in the inspector general's office either. Nothing was more compromised. Nor the bookstore (long story). Nor the bakery.

Now I drive a Lyft. There are things I like about it. I know the city well. I am somewhat free. At least I don't use Uber.

# Chapter 42

# HAPPY DAYS

A few weeks after I was fired, I saw Agnes performing at the tiny experimental theater La MaMa. She was the star of *Happy Days*, a Beckett play in which a lone woman, buried up to her neck in rubble, prattles on about her memories. Whenever she begins to sleep, a bell rings and startles her awake. The stage constructed around Agnes was supposed to resemble an Iraqi battle site with sandbags, debris, and a grenade launcher. It was the last kind of thing I wanted to see. Torture, basically. Yet I found myself strangely moved by the play. Agnes remained very, fully human onstage in inhuman conditions. I could feel her energy even as she stood endlessly trapped, suffering. I felt comforted by that, although I can't explain it. Beckett always seemed to know how smart and stupid we are at the same time.

It was the last night of the performance run so I ended up tagging along to the wrap party at KGB Bar. A few drinks into the evening, Agnes sat with me. I complimented her again.

"How does it feel?" I said.

She furrowed her brow. "To be onstage?"

"No, to be off, to be done."

"Weird," she said. "Every time I finish a play, I think, What just happened? Was it a dream? But you can't ask anyone else what happened. They can't tell you. They're unreliable witnesses. Even the other actors." She took a sip of her drink. Something with lime. Gin and tonic, I think.

"Blah!" she shouted. "Fucking fact-checker."

She hugged me. It felt like a real hug.

"I heard from Sylvia," Agnes said. "She says hi."

"'Hi'?" I repeated.

"Yeah. I got a postcard from her, from somewhere in Iowa. She mentioned you. 'If you see that fact-checker, say hello for me,'" Agnes said. "So, hello."

"Hello," I said. "What's she doing in Iowa?"

"I don't know. She didn't even send an address. She went on about Pikes Peak and then something about ancient grains. She's into wheat now."

I must have made a face.

"That's all I know," Agnes said. "Typical Sylvia: no phone, no address. 'I'll call you when I'm settled,' she wrote, and 'Sorry about the way I bailed, sorry about everything.'"

"'Sorry about everything'?"

"Aren't we all?" Agnes said.

"Some of us are," I said, "sometimes."


I headed home soon after that. I kept hearing Charles's voice in my head, barking out slugs of unchecked stories—"Maxwell/Cheney," "Parker/Swift Boat," Redonda/Meat." I kept thinking I had to check them, but I didn't. "Redonda/Meat" would never appear, and as for the "Swift Boat," we all know how that went. No fact-checker could have saved it. And I was no fact-checker.

# Acknowledgments

A word of praise goes out to all the fact-checkers who are at this moment weeding their way through the thickets of untruth: My heart is with you.

I am deeply grateful to Morgan Entrekin and Joe Brosnan for their support and to all the rest of the Grove team including Deb Seager, Judy Hottensen, David Chesanow, and Gretchen Mergenthaler. A special thanks to copy editor Logan Hill for wearing a fact-checking hat and catching some unintentional falsehoods among the many truths and fictions in this book. Joe did some fact-checking too. Indeed, YouTube was not launched until December 2005.

Chris Clemans was the perfect reader and advisor and champion through visions and revisions. Thank you, Chris. Matt Nicholas deserves an award for always responding to "is it better like this or like this?" So many others attentively read versions of this book, including Richard Larson, Leeore Schnairsohn, Kat Carlson, Nicole Callihan, Marie O'Shea, Nayana Currimbhoy, Madeleine Stein, Linell Ajello, and Colm O'Shea. Grazie mille, my friends and Fictioneers.

Thanks always to my parents, Joe and Donna Kelley. And I certainly would not have made this thing without Emily and August. Without them, nothing.